THE PAST IS NEVER
WHERE YOU LEFT IT

ISBN-13: 978-1495310607
ISBN-10: 1495310604

Acknowledgement

I would like to thank David Rice, of the Killaloe
Hedge School of Writing in Ireland, whom I was
lucky enough to meet some years back. His faith in
me as a writer and his encouragement made the
difference. I would also like to express my
deep gratitude to Frances O'Malley and Ann Murphy.
This book wouldn't have made it across the line
without either of you.

THE PAST IS NEVER WHERE YOU LEFT IT

BETTY CLARKE

QUADRIS BOOKS

FLORENCE 2012

"If you are reading this, I will be dead."

H E HEADED from his villa to the office in the building at the end of his garden, pausing for a while to take in the scent of the flowers that added to the special fragrance of a Florentine summer morning. This was a daily ritual for him when he was in Florence – an early, lingering stroll that allowed him to savour the delights of the garden he had lavished so much care on over the years, now looking beautifully mature with its groves of lemon and olive trees and a rich array of foliage bound by flower-lined, meandering paths. When he reached the office door, he turned once more to look back at the garden and decided he would definitely start soon on having a water-garden built, something that had been on his mind for a while.

The office was housed in an old mews which he had converted and extended considerably to provide a studio and to house the large range of shoes and handbags that had won him an international reputation as a designer along with as his beloved collection of shoes, bags and belts that he had collected on his worldwide travels and which provided a rich source of inspiration. Fame as a fashion designer had now been his for about fifteen years, and hardly any fashion magazine in any part of the world was published without mentioning Michael Dufay and his Avanti label, which was now almost a household name.

He stepped inside and greeted his secretary. "Morning, Stephanie, another beautiful day. On days like this I know why I spend more time here in Florence than in New York."

"You're right, Michael, but its going to get too hot and all those bloody mosquitoes, I hate them." Stephanie, an American woman in her sixties, was like a mother figure to Michael and had worked

1

for him for twelve years. She handed Michael his morning coffee. "I've left your private post on your desk. There was a large package today, all the way from Ireland." She followed him into his studio. "It must be another request for a charity donation. I know it's none of my business, but really, Michael, you're giving enough already in your yearly donations. Don't be too much of a softie."

"Thanks. I'll have a look now and, as you say, it's none of your business, so be off with you." Michael smiled as he teased her. "And thanks for the coffee. Give me a few minutes. We can go through the schedule for the next week or so, but remember, I'm not going to China again this month…it's too much of a long haul." The Chinese market had in the previous few years opened up wide to designer label handbags and shoes. They couldn't get enough of Michael's designs; their money appeared endless, and being able to display the latest label designs seemed like a badge of success to them. Michael was glad of all this, of course, but part of him sometimes wondered how people could become so obsessed by such things.

"Before I go, Michael," Stephanie said, "Mrs Relz in London was on again. She doesn't want the thirty five thousand pounds worth of shoes she paid for and left at the shop some time back but instead wants to order the new season line. She said we can keep them, throw them out, give them to staff or charity, she doesn't care. What should we do?"

"Too much money, Stephanie, these bored investment bankers' wives, too much money, too much time on their hands," Michael said. "Have them shipped to New York and hold them in storage for the auction." He was referring to the annual auction for the charity he had founded ten years previously, which had raised million of dollars for Aids research.

Stephanie left him alone in his studio. He was thinking of China when a text came through on his mobile phone,

2

Thinking of U My Michael – Luv & miss U – F XX

He sent back a similar message. After so many romantic trials and errors he had found at forty years of age the love he had sought for so long. He knew deep in his heart that this time it was the real thing. A few thousand miles separated them for work reasons at present, but soon they would be back together in New York – and then shortly afterwards would come the event they had both talked about for a long time, marriage.

Michael moved from his desk and walked around the studio to admire the view from the window. His villa, high on the hills outside Florence, had a panoramic view of the city below, where he could make out the top of Il Duomo, the famous cathedral right in the centre. Michael loved the Italian lifestyle as well as the wonderful food and had lived in Florence for many years. His next-door neighbour was a professional footballer who was treated like a god by the locals.

Michael was smiling to himself as he thought of the footballer (he had so little interest in football himself) when he absent-mindedly opened the package that had been personally addressed to him. It was marked "private and confidential", but what caught his eye most that it was not addressed to Michael Dufay, the name he had adopted early in his career to make him sound French, but to Michael Duffy, his real name.

He opened the package and found a large scrap book and an envelope marked "Michael" in small, delicate handwriting. Flicking through the scrap book, he was astounded to see newspaper and magazine cuttings about himself from 1987 right up to 2012 – practically every award ceremony he had attended, every magazine or newspaper interview he had given over the previous twenty five years. He then began to slowly turn the pages from start to finish, reading about himself in cuttings from Time, Vogue, Elle, and other magazines and seeing himself staring back from the pages in colour and black and white. There were headlines listing, along with Avanti, all major fashion labels like Prada, Louis Vuitton, Todds and Salvatore Ferragamo.

He felt a strange weakness in his legs and sat back down quickly in the large leather chair behind his desk. His breathing became faster as he tore open the letter attached to the scrap book and read it. He felt the blood draining away from his face as he read it a second time, his eyes glued to one particular phrase,

If you are reading this, I will be dead.

He called out urgently, "Stephanie...Stephanie."

"No need to shout, heard you the first time," Stephanie said as she entered with a notebook in hand. She sat opposite Michael without looking at him and was waiting with her pen at the ready when the silence made her look up.

"What's wrong, Michael? You look like you've seen a ghost. Is everything alright?" she asked in one breath. He handed Stephanie a name that he had written on a piece of paper.

"Check out this person's funeral arrangements, please. It's in my home town, Dunglass. Urgently . . . like now!" Michael's face was tired and older looking all of a sudden. "And book me a flight, I think I just might make it." Stephanie left the office immediately as Michael just sat there as if he was glued to the chair. Thirty minutes later Stephanie reappeared.

"The funeral is scheduled for tomorrow morning at the Church of Divine Mercy in Dunglass at eleven o'clock, Michael. Family flowers only but donations, if desired, to Cancer Care."

"Did you book me a flight to Dublin today?" he asked.

"Yes, Michael, it's at two o'clock. No business class available,

4

just economy, if that's okay with you? I'll organise a driver to bring you to the airport within the next hour."

"Guess I'll have to slum it and go with the cattle," Michael said in an attempt to bring some humour into his voice.

"But what about all the work here, all the meetings planned for this week, all the urgent faxes?" She was afraid of asking him but knew she had to. She watched him move towards the door, package and letter in hand. He checked his watch, knowing he wouldn't have time for his usual lunchtime meeting in the centre of Florence. His mind was racing. "God, I could do with a drink," he said to himself. It was a long time now since his last drink, almost ten years. He made a mental note to call someone he could talk to about this on his way to the airport.

"Organise me a hotel in Dublin tonight and book a driver for the day to take me down to Dunglass for the funeral in the morning, and back to the airport as soon as it's over. I want a return flight tomorrow afternoon, straight after the funeral.

"I hope you don't mind me saying, but I've never heard you mention your home town before, never mind go back for a funeral. Is it someone you know…hope it's not family? How long is it since you were home?" Stephanie asked the questions in one breath as she walked with Michael towards the villa. She could see he was visibly shaken.

"It's been many, many years since I've been back." Michael paused and looked at her. Changing the subject back to business, he said, "The Chinese will wait, stall them on the deadline, I have the designs done, not on paper but in my mind." He pointed to his head. When they reached the villa they stood together outside to go through some more business details. When Stephanie turned to head back to the office, he called after her, "By the way, Steph . . . no, it's not family, it's worse." He walked into the house and left her staring at him.

5

ON THE way to the airport he called Gerard, a Frenchman who lived in Florence and with whom he went a few times a week to meetings of Alcoholics Anonymous. They had a good chat, in which Gerard reminded him that taking a drink would put him back on the path that many years earlier had led him to almost ending his career abruptly. Michael felt more relaxed after their talk and tried to bring his attention to where he was, to calm his mind using the breathing techniques he had learned over the years. He started to breathe deeper and deeper and closed his eyes. He heard the pilot tell the crew to take their seats for take-off. Exhaling his breath as if driving out every molecule of air in his body, he felt his body and mind gently starting to relax and slow down.

Returning to Dunglass for the first time in twenty five years had opened the gates to a flood of memories. As the plane lifted itself in an arc over Florence he found his mind drifting back, right back to when he was a young man in the 1980s – a time filled with the music of Bananarama, Japan, George Michael, The Sex Pistols and Johnny Rotten. It seemed such a long time ago, in fact a different lifetime that was a million light years away from the world he now inhabited of luxurious houses, first-class travel, diva models and billionaire clients. All of it would have been the stuff of dreams back then. And yet, he remembered, it all began with one simple adventure . . .

DUNGLASS, IRELAND, 1986

MICHAEL DUFFY closed his eyes and settled himself for a short snooze, knowing that the train would take an hour to reach Dunglass. His daily slog of a journey to and from the college of art in Dun Laoghaire on the south side of Dublin, where he was about to finish his first year, always took its toll. But it was well worth it. For the past number of months he had become exposed to a whole new world of art and design, confirming him even more in his ambitions to become an artist, though he was not sure yet in what area he would like to work. And the limits of his world were about to expand further. That afternoon he had skipped lectures to go to the U.S. embassy where he had his passport stamped with a visa that would allow him to work for the summer months in New York – a chance to make some money and in a place that promised more adventure than the holiday camp near Dunglass, where he had worked the previous summer.

As the train pulled into Dunglass he decided he would check out if any of his friends were in Callan's coffee shop at the end of the main street.

Mary Rose was there with Finnuala, whose eyes lit up when Michael entered.

"Hiya, girls. You two look like those ladies of leisure who lunch every day," Michael said as he joined them.

"So what did you learn in your fancy college today, Michael?" Mary Rose asked curtly.

"I skipped college early today and headed straight to the American embassy. Look, here it is – my visa." His eyes danced as he showed them his passport.

"Oh my God, there it is, Michael, what you've wanted for a long time. No more holiday camp for you." Finnuala was thrilled for her friend, even if she would miss him.

"I think you're mad," Mary Rose said. "What's wrong with staying here and getting some money for your second year? You might not even want to come back. It's a very hard college to get into, Michael, you don't want to do anything to mess it all up." Mary Rose was in one of her condescending moods.

"Yeah, yeah, so you said a thousand times, Mary Rose. I know I was lucky to get the place, but I just happen to be a very good artist and they know that too. So no, I won't be doing anything silly. I plan to come back for my second year." Michael looked over at Finnuala. Mary Rose was not Michael's favourite company but she happened to be a friend of Finnuala's and part of the gang that hung out together. He decided to change the subject and asked if they were going to the Subterranean Disco that night.

"Course we'll be there," Finnuala said, gazing at Michael. "I'd love to have a dance or two."

"Yeah, Michael, we'll be there, although don't know why I bother," Mary Rose said.

"I wonder if the others are going," Michael said. "Were you talking to any of them?"

"I know that Cormac's working today in the holiday camp," Mary Rose told them with authority. "He got his old job back in the swimming pool area, with all the screaming kids, but he said he'll be back in time for the disco. Siobhan's doing her shift in the old people's home, and Padraig is working in the salon until seven to do the old dears' late Friday night perms and colours."

"When are you going to New York, Michael?" Finnuala asked.

"I think I'm going next week if I can get a cheap flight. Look, I'd better head off." He looked at Finnuala. "I'll see you later, about nine o'clock. Want me to call for you on the way down town?"

"Yeah, Michael, call over for me. Mary Rose will be there and we can all go down together. I'll try to siphon off some of my mother's drink." On the odd Friday night before the disco she would steal small amounts from each bottle in the drinks' cabinet and replace it with water. The end result was a potent mixture in a large plastic bottle which they all took turns to gulp down before going into the disco.

"Go handy, or your mother will notice all her drink gone. See you later." Michael smiled as he left the coffee shop.

Finnuala smiled after him, wondering what outfit she would wear later that night.

"When are you going to accept it Finnuala?" Mary Rose asked. "Michael is gay. He's not interested in you, not the way you're interested in him." Mary Rose liked to think she was an authority on all things concerning relationships.

"Well, he's bisexual actually," Finnuala answered back. "Michael told me, which means that he hasn't quite made up his mind yet, okay?" Finnuala's face was flushed. "He's over eighteen and might choose either way. I'll be there just in case, so back off, right?"

Being nasty wasn't in Finnuala's nature but she couldn't help adding, "Anyway, I don't know why you're going tonight. There'll be no guards there, not unless they're coming to arrest the rest of us normal people."

Finnuala was all too familiar with Mary Rose's obsession with snaring and marrying a man in a police uniform. She was forever talking about a guard's salary and the pension rights that went with the job. Finnuala saw the shocked look in Mary Rose's eyes and immediately regretted what she had said. She moved out of the seat and made to gather up her belongings.

"Come on, let's have a look in Woolworth's before we head home, see if there are any bargain lipsticks for tonight." Mary Rose sulked, but followed her down the main street.

THE CENTRAL Bar right in the middle of town was a busy joint whose hard-drinking regulars invariably staggered to the nearby chip-shop on their way home after closing time. Downstairs in the basement the 'Subterranean Disco' was held every Friday: a small dark cellar into which the management had scattered a few round tables and stools around a cheap wooden floor.

The club's main man was the DJ, Fat Mark, the only "out there" gay man that Michael knew in person. He was in his twenties, weighed at least twenty stone, had his head shaved and wore black eye-liner. Michael was in awe of Mark's courage to openly admit he was gay. He lived locally, but declared every Friday night that he was leaving soon for the gay club circuit in London, an announcement that everyone eventually learned to greet with indifference. He played everything from The Clash and Queen to The Sex Pistols, catering for regulars like Big John, a six-foot-five Punk rocker who dressed like his idol Johnny Rotten, with tartan trousers, size twelve Doc Martin boots and a mohair mad-red jumper. He looked menacing, but Michael had come to know him over time and knew that he was a gentle giant.

The Friday disco was the week's most important event for Michael and his friends, a chance to forget their troubles on the dance floor for a few hours, or at least to gather in a corner to complain about how much they hated their families, their lives and their one-horse town.

"You'll be twisted, Alan. Don't drink the cider so fast," Michael advised his friend.

"Mr Big Shot, giving advice on drinking now, are we?" Alan's tongue really sharpened at the edges when he was drunk.

"Leave him, Michael. Come on, let's have a dance." Finnuala grabbed Michael's hand and led him to the dance floor.

They had all arrived around the same time. Michael, Finnuala, Mary Rose and Siobhan had all walked down town to the disco after half past nine, stopping for a short while to finish off Finnuala's bottle of mixed spirits. Waiting inside were the rest of the gang – the already drunk Alan along with Cormac and Padraig

Michael had grown up with Alan in the same housing estate,

and he was used to him. But Alan was the spoiled baby in the family, born to older parents, and was accustomed to getting his own way. Michael didn't want any trouble, so he was glad to dance away with Finnuala. The other girls soon joined in. Siobhan was a great dancer, and even Mary Rose could forget herself for a full three minutes as a Freddie Mercury song played. When Michael got back to the table Cormac and Padraig were dying to ask him about New York.

"You're so lucky, Michael," Padraig said. "I wish I was going with you instead of being stuck here in this godforsaken town." .

"Why don't you come with me, Padraig? I'm sure they need hairdressers in New York." Michael took a sip of his pint of cider.

"I can't, Michael. Who'd look after my sister, with that bitch there in the house?" Padraig was referring to his stepmother Bridie, who had married his father Seamus a few years previously. She had taken an instant dislike to Padraig and his sister Martha, who was a year younger than him. Their father was oblivious to his wife's cruelty. "Last week she tied Martha to the chair with a skipping rope, said she couldn't hear the horse racing on the telly." Padraig had venom in his eyes when he talked about Bridie. "She eventually let her go, and then refused to give us any dinner because her horse didn't win the race. Imagine my stupid father married that witch . . . its unthinkable really. I should call social services." Padraig stared at them.

"Come on, Padraig, let's forget all the family hassles, just for to-night. We all have them." Michael was anxious to calm the waters.

Michael had known Padraig for years at school, and they both had met Cormac at the holiday camp where they all worked to-gether selling "kiss me quick" hats. They got on well, and although each of them was gay they didn't talk much about it. Alan, or "Contrary Alan" as Michael had nicknamed him, then joined the gang, as had Siobhan, who was Cormac's first cousin. They all suspected that Siobhan was lesbian, but no one ever said it out loud.

"Sure, look at my father," Michael said, "such an army head, so full of rules and regulations. He has my mother beaten down to a servant, a maid." Michael didn't really want to get into his own family mess, but wanted to console Padraig. "Come on, you can pick your friends but you can't pick your family."

He looked to Cormac for support, since his family set-up also wasn't exactly the "Waltons." Although Cormac adored his mother, he rarely spoke to his father, who worked all the hours God sent by day and on his occasional time-off went to Gaelic football matches. Cormac knew that he could never ever in a million years talk to his dad about sex, let alone tell him that his eldest son was gay.

Siobhan came over and sat beside Cormac. "That fat queen, I swear I'm going to kill him with a thump one of these days." Siobhan was guzzling back her drink and lighting up a cigarette at the same time.

"What's up with you Siobhan?" Cormac asked.. "Who are you going to kill this week?" Everyone was used to Siobhan's aggressive behaviour, and knew that a night out wouldn't be complete for her without an altercation with someone. She was a very strong young woman and played on the local women's rugby team. Nobody had any doubts that she could hold her own.

"That DJ, Fat Mark. I'll Fat Mark him. I'll give him a fat lip if he doesn't play that request for me. He forgot last week. She's my hero, and I love her." Everyone knew about her obsession with K D Lang, the gay American singer.

"Looks like everyone is in great form tonight," Michael said sarcastically, looking around and wondering how many hours it would be until he was on that plane for New York. The music changed, and the "slow set" started.

12

"Come on, Michael, dance with me. It's 'The Power of Love', our favourite." Finnuala was on her feet in a flash, grabbing Michael's hand to lead him to the dance floor. Michael knew Finnuala had a crush on him. She had told him so nearly every Friday night on the way home from the disco when she was drunk. He followed her, onto the dance floor, knowing it was going to be difficult that night to escape her advances. He had explained to her many times that although he did love her, he loved her like a sister and nothing else. She had a tight grip on Michael as they danced to the slow, romantic music. The alcohol had affected her and she was feeling light-headed and a bit dizzy.

"I'm going to miss you, Michael," she whispered as she placed her arms around his neck to draw him closer. "Who will I talk to when you're in America?"

"You'll be fine. I'll write to you, and it's only for a few months, Finnuala. Sure, you'll be going off to work in Dublin in September yourself … you'll get the call from the civil service by then."

"But it won't be the same without you, Michael." She seemed beyond consoling as she buried her head in his chest. Michael casually glanced back to their table. He had just noticed Fat Mark walking around, as he usually did during the slow set. Just then he heard a crash of glasses and looked over to see Siobhan lunging towards Fat Mark. Michael released himself from a dazed Finnuala and ran over. Cormac and Padraig had grabbed hold of Siobhan and were just about managing to hold her back.

Fat Mark was screaming at the top of his voice. "Get this wild bitch out of my club. Now! Just because I wouldn't play her stupid request. Someone get this wild lunatic off me."

"You fat queen," Siobhan screamed back, "you should know by now not to cross me." Before she could finish her tirade two bouncers pounced and hauled her quickly to the door. Cormac followed them.

"Look, you stay on and enjoy the night, it's too early," he said to the others. "I'll bring her back to my house and fill her with coffee before she can head home. I've the number of a new taxi I got a few times…Pearse, he'll be on the taxi rank." Cormac was drinking down his pint of shandy as he steered Siobhan out onto the street.

"I'll come with you, Cormac," Michael said and turned around to Finnuala. "Sorry, but I better head off with Cormac and see that Siobhan is okay. We'll all meet up tomorrow in Callan's around three." Michael ran after Cormac and Siobhan. Finnuala and Mary Rose were helping the barman to pick up the broken glasses. Alan was ranting and raving about his drink being spilled and cursing away to himself. But no one was listening and the girls headed to the toilets. Finnuala went straight to a toilet bowl to vomit her guts up and then cried her eyes out. The night was ruined now that Michael was gone. Mary Rose busied herself, re-applying makeup at the mirror and thanking God Finnuala was nowhere near her new outfit when she got sick. As she put on her red lipstick she thought of next week and the rumour she had heard of the new batch of guards coming to town.

MICHAEL PUT on the kettle to make Siobhan another strong cup of coffee with plenty of sugar. After the fracas at the disco he and Cormac had managed to bundle Siobhan into a taxi, but Michael then got out with her at her house, leaving Cormac to continue his journey alone.

Siobhan's temper had worn off, and now the tears flowed as she sat at the kitchen table. "I just don't fit in around here, Michael," she said softly, not wanting to wake her father upstairs. "I never have. I hate being different than the others. It's harder than being straight."

14

"Here, drink this." He placed the second coffee in front of her, which she sipped slowly. "I know it's difficult, Siobhan, but you drink too much. It all comes out when you're drunk. You should lay off it."

"I feel like a big fish in a small bowl, and there's a big world out there. I'm trapped here, Michael, trapped." Siobhan pointed upwards to her sleeping dad upstairs.

"Come with me to New York, Siobhan," Michael said looking intently at her. "Save up your wages and come out in a few weeks. I'll have a place sorted by then. Even if it's only for a month, come anyway."

Blowing her nose with a piece of kitchen roll, she gulped. "I can't Michael, I can't leave my dad on his own. I'm trapped here since Mam died."

Michael sat in silence as he nodded. He knew that her mother's death from cancer five years ago had taken its toll. Whenever she was drunk her loneliness and loss overflowed.

"Padraig wants me to go to Dublin with him next week, to try this gay bar." Siobhan forced a smile. "I suppose it would be a small escape, some hope on the horizon." She stalled on the words.

"Where there is life, there is hope." Michael smiled at her, grateful that her tears had stopped. "Look, I'd better get going." Michael stood up and grabbed his coat from the back of the chair. "I'll talk to you before I go, Siobhan. Get to bed, have some rest and tomorrow you'll feel better. As I said, lay off the drink, and the offer still stands. You can come to New York if you change your mind in a couple of weeks."

They made direct eye contact, both knowing that Siobhan wouldn't take up Michael's offer, but that it would help her knowing it was there.

CORMAC COULD hear the sound of the high waves crashing on Faunstown beach as he lay in bed in the cramped bedroom of the mobile home. The man lying next to him took up most of the room in the double bed. Cormac observed that his thick-black body hair went all over his chest, his neck and all the way down his back. The man's name was Pearse, and their encounter had started like a bolt of lightening when Cormac found himself alone in the taxi after Michael and Siobhan got out. He was shocked when Pearse made the first move by placing his hand on Cormac's thigh. The attraction between them was instant, an electric force greater than anything he had ever felt.

"Fancy some fun?" were the words Pearse had whispered to Cormac. Afraid to speak, Cormac just nodded yes in agreement. Pearse drove the taxi frantically to his brother's mobile home where their hungry, urgent kisses were followed by an explosive release. Cormac now understood what "mind-blowing sex" really felt like.

Pearse pulled himself up and swung his legs out on the floor to sit at the edge of the bed. He looked sideways at Cormac. "You know who I am, don't you?"

"Sure I do," Cormac said. "You're going out with Jackie. My friend Padraig works for Dinah, Jackie's mother, in the hair salon."

"We both know Dunglass is very small," Pearse said as he lay down again and faced Cormac. "What age are you? I hope you're not under-age or I'll be put in jail."

"I'm twenty-one years of age, thank you very much. I just have a young face."

"You'll be glad of a young face when you get to my age."

"And what age is that?"

"Well, I'm ten years older than you, so you do the maths. C'mon we better go home." Pearse hauled himself out of the bed and looked down at Cormac as he started to dress. Cormac held his breath, afraid to say anything. He wondered if he might dare to hope that he would see Pearse again.

"I've never done this before," Pearse said. "It's the first time I've been with a man. But you're different."

"You're very kind to say that," Cormac said, gushing as he looked at Pearse. He was thrilled that this older, more sophisticated man of the world had picked him.

"C'mon, we'll go back and I'll drop you near the church. It was great, Cormac, and I hope we can do it again soon."

"Sure, sure whenever you think," Cormac said and then stopped himself, not wanting to appear too needy.

"We will, we will," Pearse said as he made his way towards the door. He looked back at Cormac's innocent face and felt a great deal of satisfaction. The one thing he was good at in life was sex, and practice made perfect.

NEW YORK, 1986

MICHAEL'S MIND was racing with doubts about the loose arrangements he had made through a college friend as he travelled by cab from JFK Airport to the centre of Manhattan. A man called Ernie, Times Square, and Doyle's Diner at nine o'clock, he silently chanted. He had allowed himself the luxury of a cab from the airport just to make sure he didn't get lost; it also gave him the time to take in the enormity of his new surroundings: the streets, the buildings, the huge numbers of people scattering in all directions. He had just flown three thousand miles from home, his first time on a plane, his first time out of Ireland, and he prayed that this guy Ernie would show up or he was in big trouble.

The cab deposited him at Times Square and Michael soon

found Doyle's Diner, where he stood outside, trying to look as natural as possible. His fingers were going numb with the death's grip he had on his hold-all. He tried to paint a confident look on his face to camouflage the jumpy, edgy anxiety building in his stomach. After ten minutes he noticed a man coming towards him, strutting like John Travolta in "Saturday Night Fever". He was tall and skinny and looked about thirty. Sure enough, he walked over towards Michael.

"Hi, you must be that kid Michael from Ireland. I'm Ernie," the man said. It must be the hold-all, Michael thought, not aware of the naïve, lost look all over his face. "You gonna take the room at my apartment, I believe," Ernie said as he extended his right hand to shake Michael's, taking his holdall with his left, all in one fluid movement. "Got to warn you, kid, it gets mighty hot here in July." Michael noticed that Ernie's New York twang didn't completely hide the lilt of a Cork accent. He followed after him down the street like a child.

"We'll take the subway from here." Ernie led the way as they headed towards the nearest subway. He explained that his apartment was in Williamsburg, Brooklyn, which was just two stops out of Manhattan on the L train. As they sat on the train Ernie explained all about Manhattan. "It's uptown and downtown baby, you can't go wrong. It's all based on blocks." Ernie pointed out things to Michael as if they were walking along a street instead of being on an underground train. His facial expressions were very dramatic, but Michael followed and took note of everything he said. "Manhattan is where the action is, if you get my drift," Ernie explained. "Brooklyn's not bad, it's half the rent, but Manhattan is where the in-crowd live. I'm gonna live there by this time next year."

When they got to his apartment he gave Michael his life story within ten minutes. He was in his early thirties and had been raised in Cork city but had lived in New York for the past five years. He worked in "Secret Delights", a sex shop, which gave him enough money to buy new outfits to wear clubbing in the gay club scene, which he did most nights. "I ain't a hand-holding tourist minder to you kid, okay, so here's your keys and welcome to New York City," he said ceremoniously. "You've gotta learn to make it on your own. The rent for your room is two hundred dollars a month, due on the first of every month."

Panic hit Michael instantly; the total amount of money he had was five hundred dollars, all held in a small string purse around his neck hidden by his shirt.

"There's some bread and cheese in the refrigerator, but just this once, just to welcome you. From here on in you buy your own food." A smile appeared on Ernie face. "Ain't no back doors with me, Michael, what you see is what you get. Help yourself to coffee and make a sandwich, I'm off out clubbing tonight." Ernie disappeared into his own bedroom, leaving Michael alone in the small kitchen. Within ten minutes he reappeared and introduced Glam Ernie.

"Meet Glam Ernie. You like it, Michael?" Ernie pointed to the new dress he had bought that day in Chinatown, a full-length, canary-yellow satin dress with a deep plunging neckline. It was the first time Michael had ever seen a man dressed up as a woman right before him in the flesh. He stared at Ernie's hairless shiny chest, his ruby-red lips pouting and his make-up, which had been applied to perfection. Wearing a long blond wig, Ernie could almost pass for a woman, Michael thought, except for his six-foot-two frame and large, protruding Adam's apple. The huge white feather fan in Ernie's hands gave the desired dramatic effect and finished off the whole outfit. Michael was afraid at first to speak but eventually told Ernie how brilliant he looked. His eyes widened as Ernie then showed off his silver knee-high platform boots.

"What size are they Ernie? I didn't know you could get boots like that in men's sizes, thought they were only for women?"

"I'm a size eleven." Ernie was thrilled with Michael's interest in his boots and pulled up his dress to show his prized platforms at their best. "You can buy anything you want here in New York, Michael, they have them right up to size sixteen in men's sizes for – how shall I put it? – the larger man." Ernie had a glint in his eye as he spoke. "And if I'm lucky I'll get my hands on one of those larger men before the night is out." Ernie grabbed his silver clutch bag and headed towards the door. "Heading to the Palladium tonight, baby, don't wait up."

Michael was gobsmacked, wondering what lay ahead for him over the next three months. Dragging his hold-all to his small bedroom off the kitchen he threw himself on the single bed. A flood of thoughts hit him as he lay there trying to sleep. Did Ernie like women, or men or both? Was he a transsexual? Why dress like a woman if you were a man? If Michael decided to be a fully fledged gay man, would he have to start dressing up as a woman, to attract the right man? The questions seemed endless, but there was no one right answer. It appeared so complicated to be gay, to be Irish and to be in New York. It was all too much like hard work to think about it right now, so Michael let the panic, fear and excitement subside. Eventually the jet-lag overtook him, and sleep finally came.

Next morning Michael awoke to the sound of loud music and a woman singing. For a split second he thought he was back in Ireland, until he remembered the flight to New York, the apartment and Glam Ernie. Like a flash it registered with him. While chattering along the sidewalk, Ernie had announced that his idol was Audrey Hepburn and that he was Ernie AKA Audrey. Michael realised that the woman singing was Audrey Hepburn from the movie "Breakfast at Tiffany's". Dragging on his clothes, he walked into the kitchen of the tiny apartment. He tried not to stare at Ernie's full-length red satin dressing gown with Chinese pictures and writing on the back. He was busy frying eggs on the gas cooker.

"If you've got company, Ernie, I won't be long. Just let me grab a drink of water and I'll be off looking for a job." Michael was apologising when a small red-haired young woman appeared out of the bathroom.

"It was no 'all-nighter' last night, sweetie," Ernie said. "I got home around two o'clock. Suppose you can't win them all. You'll have to come clubbing with me, Michael, when you get settled in. Need to head in shortly, got to open up the shop as the boss is away. He's gone home to China and there are deliveries due today and they're even extending the shop." As Ernie rambled on, the girl with the friendly face extended her hand to Michael.

"Don't worry, I'm not Ernie's company, I'm Pearl from upstairs. I came down to check on Ernie's gallivanting last night." She spoke with a strong Cork accent.

"Hi, I'm Michael. I'm here for the summer," Michael explained. "I need to find a job now and get settled in."

"If you're looking for work you could try the restaurant on Carmine Street, downtown in Little Italy," Pearl said. "I heard they're hiring. Isabella does the hiring, I think. It's the coolest restaurant down that area." Pearl headed towards the door. "Anyone will show you, talk to you again, Michael. I'm only upstairs if you need anything."

Opening the door Pearl paused and smiled. "And don't mind Audrey, you'll get used to her singing. You'd better, because Ernie plays nothing else." She was gone. Ernie wrote down the address of the restaurant for Michael, together with a list of the subway and street connections.

After searching for a few hours, Michael found the restaurant

21

and was immediately blown away as he stepped into its dimly lit interior. All the inside walls had maps of the world painted like a scene from "The Godfather". He counted ten large round tables with chairs placed in the centre of the room, each covered with red and white check tablecloths. Another ten private booths were positioned on the back wall of the restaurant. Michael asked to speak to Isabella, who came to the front desk. She told him there were no positions at the moment, but did take his name. Michael left feeling deflated but vowed to go back, which he did, every day for five days around eleven o'clock – "not too early, not too late" – and asked to speak to Isabella.

On the fifth day she took pity on him, telling him that she didn't have any positions as a waiter, but he could help wash up in the kitchen, starting that night. Michael floated happily back on the subway to tell Pearl his good news. They shared a coffee most days in her apartment or in the diner on the corner of the street. He felt so good he bought a bunch of postcards and stamps on the way home. He wrote a few and posted them to Ireland before heading back to the apartment to find Pearl and get ready for work.

Postcard of Manhattan Island, with twin towers, sky-scrapers in the distance surrounded by water
Dear Finnuala, Finally got here. Very hot. Got a job today in an Italian Restaurant. Start tonight. Everything is huge, lots of fat people everywhere. Having a great time. Miss the gang. Write me at above address if you can. Wish you were here. Michael x

Postcard – Picture of Bay and Statue of Liberty
Dear Mam & Dad, Hope you are keeping well at home. I am working hard in New York. I got a job in an Italian restaurant. I get fed there. I'm trying to save some money, but can't send home

22

any yet. I am sharing a flat with a nice boy from Cork who works very hard in a busy shop and who loves singing Audrey Hepburn songs, just like granny. I go out the odd time and plan to go to Mass this Sunday. Will write again soon. Michael x

POSTCARD — PICTURE OF A VERY MUSCULAR, VEINS BULGING, BLONDE WOMAN DRESSED IN A TINY BIKINI

Dear Siobhan, Thought you'd like this picture! Am loving New York, strange by day but even wilder by night. Clubs and discos huge. I walk in Central Park most days, it's like a movie set. Imagine they buy water to drink from a bottle? AND 'jog', or run around for the exercise!! Crazy, but you'd love it. Write me & wish you were here. Michael xx

BY THE time three weeks had passed, Michael's days had fallen into such a pattern that it seemed sometimes he had been doing it all his life. And he was even becoming used to the city's sweltering heat and humidity. He would do his shift washing dishes in the restaurant most nights until about midnight and then come home by the subway. During the day he either got the train into Manhattan to explore the city on foot or spent lots of time hanging out with Pearl in her apartment. They had become good friends and always found lots to talk about. Pearl had problems at home, mostly with her mother who drank too much. Her worst fear was to get stuck with a layabout husband and brats of children, like her two sisters.

She worked in a bar and restaurant in Brooklyn not too far away from their apartment block where she earned lots of tips because of her friendly, smiling face. What she wanted most of all was to be a writer and she had started taking classes in creative writing in a Brooklyn college, as well as writing articles for local newspapers and magazines. She hadn't received much money for these, but she had applied to a college in London to study journalism and needed them for a portfolio.

The college she attended had organised a fashion show and Michael had gone along with her for the fun. He was enthralled by all the designs, so different from what he had seen at student shows back home, but what caught his eye most were the shoes. Some of the models were wearing what he later discovered were called Brothel Creepers. Michael was fascinated by them. While Pearl was taking notes, all he wanted to do was sketch the shoes which seemed so special with their straps and huge soles. He talked to Pearl about them all the way home and then back at the apartment.

It was as if a light bulb had gone on in his head. He had given some thought to being a fashion designer, but what excited him most of all now was the possibility of working with shoes.

Pearl told him he should start browsing through the up-market shops just a couple of blocks from his work. The following day he got off the subway a few blocks early and walked towards Little Italy to explore all the huge window displays. One in particular caught his eye, a display of summer shoes and sandals. They were mounted on a shiny gold stand with extra lighting shining on the shoes, which made them even more appealing. He was thinking about heels,and the height of each heel on the shoe when out of nowhere he heard a voice.

"Slow blow ball lick…fifty dollars?" Michael turned around to see an old-looking oriental woman who couldn't have been more than five feet tall. Well dressed, she looked like one of the many tourists walking in the area. Michael thought she had asked him for directions.

"Sorry…eh…miss, I'm not from around here…" Michael started to say and was about to tell her to go up to the policeman on the corner when she interrupted him.

"Slow blow, slow blow ball lick, fifty dollars. You like some boy?" Me have bones, brittle bones, so doctor say no sex…so no full sex boy…bad for me…but me give very good blow job."

Michael understood now and was gripped by panic. He stared at her smiling grandmotherly face and somehow managed to find his voice again.

"No, no honestly…thanks very much…not today, thanks." He started to move away, but she stepped after him, softly saying to him in her broken English:

"You come another day, boy. I here every day between two and five, we go to my apartment…not far. You come back then, my child. Maybe I see you another day." She continued to smile as she slowly walked off, while Michael left as fast as he could without having to break into a run. Although he was too early for his shift he went straight to the restaurant where he told Isabella what had happened. Isabella in turn told the rest of the kitchen staff, who fell about laughing. Everyone thought it was hilarious that Michael was so naïve and innocent.

"Maybe she likes her men young, Michael." Isabella was smiling as the others laughed heartily. "Young, fresh meat, it puts a whole new slant on the saying, 'your granny loves you baby', doesn't it Michael?"

As he went through hundreds of dishes that night, he couldn't help but smile to himself. What a story to tell his friends. When he finished his shift around midnight he called into the all-night store on the corner where he searched through the rows of cards and postcards, finally picking a picture post card of the American top boy band 'New Handful' – four young men with beautiful bodies and hairless chests. Michael wrote it to Padraig, addressing it to the salon rather than to his home.

POSTCARD TO PADRAIG – 'NEW HANDFUL' – TOP BOY BAND
USA 1986

Hi Padraig, Love New York - Bigger and bolder each day.
Its mind blowing and intense!!!! Am having a ball - Just had to
beat off an eighty year old pro offering B J. Should have told her
you'd do the job for nothing!!!! Wish you were here – you would
love it. Write me. Michael x

"YOU LIKE working at that restaurant,?" the old barber asked as
he trimmed Michael's hair. Michael sat in the barber's huge old
leather chair, savouring the smell of fresh soap, shaving foam and
freshly washed towels that hit him every time he entered the small
shop – so small it allowed only room to cut one person's hair at a
time. There was a small wooden bench against the wall together
with a table on which magazines were placed. They were mostly
in Italian, so Michael didn't understand them. But he didn't have
to wait today as he was the only customer in the shop.

"I've been working there nearly four weeks now and get shifts
mostly at the weekend," Michael answered. "I'm heading there
after the hair cut." Michael liked the look of the old Italian. At
seventy-five years of age, Fausto had told him his life story and
how he had come to New York as a teenager nearly sixty years ago.
The years were flying by, and now his hair was grey and bushy.
He ran the barber shop on his own and lived in a small apartment
overhead. Fausto's hands were small and twisted from arthritis,
and he walked with a limp, but his eyes were still blue and full of
life. He had told Michael his wife died nearly five years ago, and
his children had busy lives so he rarely saw them these days, only
on occasions - usually funerals.

"I came to America like you, Michael, full of hopes and
dreams. They don't always happen, but as long as I can cut hair

and chat with my customers I am happy." Fausto smiled at Michael. "And dancing, Michael, once I can still go to my dances on Sunday afternoons at Hailey's Hall, a few blocks away, I am still alive! Do you like to dance, Michael?"

Michael smiled to himself. He was going dancing after his shift at the restaurant with Glam Ernie, but it was a kind of dancing that Fausto could never have imagined. He had been clubbing with Ernie many times since he arrived in New York, and tonight they were hitting the Palladium again where "Dock Yard Doris" was on the bill. Michael had never been to a live drag queen show, so tonight would be a first for him. He had met an amazing man called Paulo at one of these nights out. Something he couldn't mention to the old man was that he had explosive urgent sex with Paulo back at Paulo's apartment within two hours of meeting. The dark and sultry Paulo might be Italian, but that was the only thing he would have in common with Fausto. Feeling cowardly, he said, "Yes Fausto we have dancing in Ireland, we like to dance there. We have what we call 'Ceilis', Irish dancing for both boys and girls." He paid Fausto and said, "Enjoy the dancing tomorrow and I bet you all the lovely ladies will be dragging you up onto the floor for the ladies choice."

"You be a good boy, Michael." Fausto lowered his voice to a whisper, even though there was no one else in the shop. Walking over to Michael he whispered in his ear: "Take my advice. Michael. Be careful of the Lombardi family, where you work. They are not quite what they seem." Pausing, Fausto started to say something else but stopped himself. Turning, he bid Michael goodbye. "Just you be careful, Michael...Ciao, and call for coffee anytime."

Michael left the small shop and headed towards the restaurant. He thought it a bit strange; it seemed as if Fausto was about to say something, but he quickly dismissed it as he walked towards the restaurant thinking of the night ahead with Ernie and his friends after he finished work. He had feeling that, as Ernie had promised, it would be a night to remember.

MICHAEL HAD been promoted to collecting glasses and delph from the tables. He liked being able to see the well-heeled customers and their lavish style of dressing.

At the beginning of his shift Isabella had handed him a crisp clean white shirt. "Every night come in wearing this clean and ironed and we'll see how you get on," she said. "Maybe we might make a waiter out of you yet." Michael reckoned that Isabella was the other side of fifty. The heavy dark eye-liner and skirts that were too short had prompted whispered comments in the kitchen; "mutton dressed as lamb" was one he heard frequently. Isabella had been unlucky in love with a constant stream of short term disastrous flings, Michael was told, mostly with married men. She was a hardened New Yorker, one not to be messed with. Michael liked her, but he was a little afraid of her and her demands.

"Stop eating the leftovers, Maria! For Christ sake, are you some kind of a vacuum cleaner? We won't have an apron big enough to fit you." Isabella was shouting at the cook as Michael brought in another batch of empty glasses on a tray. Isabella was right. Every time Michael came into the kitchen Maria was eating something. She was the fattest woman he had ever seen. She must have weighed twenty five stone, with her chest, waist and hips all running down in one straight line. She had a very bad habit of eating what the customers left on their plates before the wash-up.

"It's all going to waste, Isabella, mind your own business," Maria shouted back angrily.. "You don't own this place, you middle-aged tart. I don't like your tone."

"It's not your food," Isabella said. "I'll talk to Francesca the next time she's here. She won't like you talking to family like that." Michael listened as the two women threw themselves into a full-scale row and realised just how much they hated each other. He wasn't sure of the family dynamics, but all the Italians in the kitchen seemed to be related somehow to the Lombardi family, the owners. Within a flash, the six-foot-four doorman Stefano appeared menacingly in the kitchen. He started shouting in Italian, and both women immediately fell silent.

"Get back to work now, the show is over," Stefano shouted to everyone else in the kitchen. Michael ran back out into the restaurant as quick as he could to shine the glasses on the shelves of the small bar. Christ, he thought, I could do with a drink. He quietly selected the first clear bottle he could find on the shelf, not knowing if it was vodka or gin, and poured it into a glass, stashing it on the tray. He cleared away dirty plates from the tables and, as he was heading towards the kitchen, he had an opportunity to put the glass to his head, swallowing the liquid in one gulp. He was getting used to his secret drinking; it helped to calm the nervous feeling in the pit of his stomach and always helped his shift to go by faster.

"THERE, IT'S posted," Michael said to Pearl, kissing the large envelope before dropping it into the mail box.

Pearl had spent a few days helping Michael, first by accompanying him to the library to look up details from books listing art and design colleges in London and to see if any of them specialised in shoe design. Together they found Wordwaines in Hackney, part of the London College of Fashion. Michael had spent many hours sketching, designing different types of heels, soles, buckles and straps, and finally drew a number of prototypes. Pearl helped him type out a letter of application to the college for September, and now the whole package was now on route to London.

"What about your college in Dublin, Michael?" Pearl had asked during their research. "Don't you want to finish your course there?"

"If I get a place in London, I'll take it. I don't think I can live at home in Dunglass after being here in New York…its just such freedom." Michael paused. "Then again, I can't imagine my mother, or rather my dad, accepting me if I came right out and told them that I prefer men to women." Michael found it easy to talk to Pearl, just like he had with Finnuala. He loved women's company, talking to them, hanging out with them. He just never wanted to rip their clothes off – that urge only happened to him with men.

"What's it like being gay, Michael? What about this girl, Finnuala, at home? Doesn't she think you two might be an item?"

"I don't know, Pearl. I do love her…like a sister or friend, but she has other ideas…and I, well I tried to fit in at home…but I didn't lead her astray, just the odd kiss, nothing more, honestly."

"And where does Paulo fit into all this? You seem to be pretty smitten with him? Ernie says he is a 'fine thing', as we say in Cork."

Michael didn't want to talk about Paulo so he turned the conversation to her own love life.

"What about you, Pearl? Why don't you have any boyfriends chasing you? You're gorgeous, you should have a queue at your front door." Michael looked at her. "We can go to a straight club some night if you want. Hell, Pearl, get out there and meet someone, some nice guy. You need to get laid." Michael thought he was being helpful.

"Getting laid by a different fella every night of the week is something men do, Michael…especially if they're like Ernie. Lets face it, we both know Ernie's track record…he doesn't bother with names at this stage, in case he mixes them up." Pearl looked

30

a bit sad as she spoke. "I want someone to love me, Michael, really love me...all of me, not just my body. Maybe it's a woman thing, but I'd like someone who'll hang around after the sex." She looked at him.

"Well maybe this monogamy is a woman thing, because all I see in the clubs is sex, sex and more sex. The guys have sex in the toilets, and there's even a dark room at the back of the club... which I refuse to go to...well, at the moment." Michael laughed. He wasn't being judgemental, but since he had met Paulo they had continued to have great sex, always back at Paulo's expensive apartment. "Look, Pearl, before this turns into a deep and meaningful conversation like the ones we usually have in your apartment after two bottles of cider, just let's say I've always known I was gay...from when I was about ten or twelve years of age." Michael paused to sip his coffee, then continued. "I was always different from the other boys on our street at home. I didn't like football, always preferred plants and being in the garden, then when I hit puberty, well, it was boys I fancied rather than girls. It's just as simple as that, Pearl, honestly. I'm a normal fella with feelings,... but I'm gay." Pearl looked at him. He was so easy to talk to and hang out with; such a pity most straight men were not like gay men.

When they finished their coffee they walked for a few blocks. Michael wanted to show Pearl a new second-hand shop he had discovered.

"Fascinating," whispered Pearl as they wandered around. As they headed towards the shoe racks at the back of the store, Michael nudged Pearl to look in the direction of two female customers lingering at the evening dresses rail.

"Men," Michael whispered, "they are two men, waiting to have the operation, the sex change." His voice was barely audible. "Close your mouth, Pearl," Michael added as she stared at the two small skinny figures, each with shoulder-length peroxide blonde hair. "They're waiting for the chop," Michael whispered again, making an up and down movement with his hands towards his groin. Pearl watched them out of the corner of her eye as they worked their way through the rails, picking out dresses before heading to the fitting rooms.

"Which fitting room do they go into, the men's or the women's?" Pearl whispered to Michael innocently.

"The women's of course, dumb-dumb. Come on, let's get out of here before you swallow them up with your open mouth." They left the shop and were still giggling as they made their way along the street. "They're regular customers. I've seen them each time I've been in the shop. The only give-away is the Adam's Apple, and I heard that with the right hormones that can be fixed too. You should write an article on it, Pearl, it would be fascinating." Michael felt very world-wise all of a sudden, as if he had inside track knowledge. "Come on, I'll introduce you to Fausto, my barber friend I was telling you about. Reminds me of my granddad at home when he was alive."

After a few blocks they arrived outside Fausto's. Michael almost bumped into Stefano from the restaurant making his way out of the shop. He could smell his breath as their eyes met and locked for a few seconds before Stefano turned abruptly to head off down the street. It made a chill run down Michael's spine. Fausto was alone in the shop; he looked flushed in the face and disturbed. He tried a weak smile at Michael and did shake hands with Pearl, but Michael knew that something was wrong.

"I am sorry, Michael, but you catch me on a bad day today. I must close up early, I go to sleep now. Sorry, Michael, you bring your lady friend for me to meet another day and I make us some good Italian coffee...ciao." Fausto was ushering them to the door. Pearl stepped outside, but Michael lingered to ask the old man what was wrong. "Is it something to do with that man Stefano? Did he hurt you, Fausto, do you want me to call the cops?"

"Michael, you are so young, so naive...make matters worse. Go with your girl...be careful of that Lombardi family. Stefano is a nasty piece of work. Fausto paused for breath and then continued "Today I need rest, I'm tired. You call again, my son...again." Fausto closed the door after Michael and moved the "closed" sign over the front door.

"You know the strangest of people, Michael. In all the time I've been here...I've led such a sheltered life," Pearl said after he told her about Stefano. "Bet you it's protection money. Isn't that what the Mafia specialise in?" Pearl was enthralled, her mind going into overdrive. They sat close together on the subway, shoulders touching, as they made their way home. Pearl's mind was full of excitement, busily shaping in her mind a novel using all of the characters they had encountered in the city that day. Michael's mind was troubled. He knew Fausto was in some kind of danger but didn't know how he could help.

Michael had worked at the restaurant for six weeks and was now getting five or six shifts per week. He felt like part of the furniture and loved the buzz of the place. Maria, the cook, had started to join Michael for a smoke in the lane-way at the back of the kitchen in an attempt to curb her compulsive eating. It wasn't really working; after a few pulls she got bored and would run back to the kitchen to retrieve a lump of cooked meat or half a cheese cake and scuttle back out to the alley to rejoin Michael.

"Francesca is due in tonight. She's just back from the family holiday home in Italy," she told Michael between mouthfuls from a small leg of lamb that she had retrieved from the back of the refrigerator. Michael liked Maria, who was kind but a bit sad. Her only joy in life was her food. Her equally fat husband Alvro came to collect her each night after her shift, but he seemed oblivious to her; according to others in the kitchen, he was more interested in her wage packet to fund his gambling.

"What's she like then, this Francesca, Maria?" Michael had learned fast to ask questions and then wait, just to listen. "Say nothing, till you hear more, then say nothing" was one of his granny's wise sayings.

"Francesca is the very beautiful, only daughter of Luca Lombardi." Maria munched on her lamb as she talked. Michael puffed on his cigarette, giving her time. "She'll make a good business woman herself someday. She's just finished some important business school degree thing down in Wall Street and she plans to take over the family business, this restaurant, the club and the other bits and pieces, when the time is right." Maria paused to attack her leg of lamb again. "She's engaged to be married next year, but I don't like the look of her boyfriend. Something is not quite right there, believe me. He's a good looking boy…too good looking if you ask me." Maria was related in some way or other to the Lombardi family, but now was not the time to complicate the issue, so Michael continued with another question.

"What about Stefano? Is he Francesa's uncle or is he related some way?"

"Not her uncle, but a cousin of her father's…came here to New York straight from Naples, five years ago. He had to get out of Italy in a hurry. Now he's the money man in the family . . . well, one of them." Maria was by now nearly finished her leg of lamb, her hands and face greasy with pieces of meat stuck to her face. Michael looked away to finish his cigarette. "I've said too much already. Keep that to yourself, Michael. Now run along and get me that meringue desert…top shelf, on the right, way at the back, behind the jar of pickles, bring it out here quick as you can. I've five minutes left on my break, hurry." Maria was talking like an addict about her next fix.

34

Michael ran back into the kitchen to retrieve the dessert and grabbed a spoon, not quite sure if Maria needed it or if she would just use her hands. He then left Maria to her eating and went straight back through the kitchen to the tables in the restaurant.

Sure enough, Francesca made her grand entrance later in the evening with her mother Viviane. The two women dined together in a corner, both tanned and with an aura of elegance that seemed straight out of a glossy magazine. Michael managed to manoeuvre his way over to the table to collect the glasses and got a glimpse of the dazzling diamond engagement ring on Francesca's left hand. He couldn't delay too long, but managed to notice the quality of the fabric of both their outfits. Designer all the way. Although Stefano was hovering nearby like a bad smell, Michael took a chance and dropped a napkin on the floor and bent down to retrieve it in order to get a good view of their shoes. Francesca had a pair of six-inch black patent high-heels with red soles, while her mother had opted for a more demure navy court shoe matching her navy and white Valentino dress suit. He did a quick calculation of what they would have cost and, still feeling dazzled by their wealth, went back to work the other tables.

MICHAEL MET Paulo while out clubbing one night with Ernie. He had been standing at the bar, happy just to gaze at the dancers, when he heard someone say something to him. Turning around, he was greeted by a friendly smile from Paulo who moved closer and placed his arm gently around Michael's waist. They chatted for a few moments, allowing Michael to take in the body that stood close to him: muscular and toned to perfection, eyes as dark as his jet-black hair. The impact was overwhelming; never before had Michael felt such an urgent desire to touch and explore someone else's body. Michael could see nobody else in the room. There were hundreds of others around them dancing, but it was as if he and Paulo were the only two there.

Each time they had met since ended in the same way: explosive, deeply satisfying, almost draining sex back at Paulo's apartment in Manhattan, after which Michael's mind was emptied and his body felt like the surface of a calm, clear lake. Michael was shocked, almost frightened, by the effect that Paulo had on him, but he tried to play down these feelings whenever he was around him.

Following one such session as they lay entangled together on Paulo's bed, Michael was beginning to drift into a light sleep when he heard Paulo say:

"You know, Michael, I have a girlfriend…I would say you have heard by now." Paulo wasn't one for many words, so Michael was a bit taken aback that he had instigated such honesty.

"Listen, Paulo, I understand. We're both adults, we can do what we want with our own bodies." Michael was trying to sound mature, fighting against the bile of jealousy building up at the back of his throat. Ernie had already warned him that Paulo was a player in the club scene.

"I suppose you would call me bisexual, going with men and women, but really I prefer men…men like you Michael, so beautiful inside and out." Paulo kissed Michael's nose tenderly, returning his head to lie gently on Michael's chest.

"Thanks, Paulo. You don't know how good that makes me feel, but can I ask you something?" Michael was afraid, but he had wanted to ask Paulo something since they had first met.

"Ask me anything, Michael. I like you, you mean a lot to me." Paulo moved up in the bed to rest his head on a pillow and stared straight through his sea-blue coloured eyes.

"Why can't you be openly gay, I mean here in New York? Isn't it okay to be gay here? It seems to me to be a big city where everyone is free to be themselves." Paulo gave a sarcastic laugh and took a cigarette from the packet on the locker. He sat up in silence, leaning back on the leather wall-mounted headboard. He lit the cigarette, inhaled deeply and answered.

"Are you crazy? You really are a little boy all the way from Ireland, Michael." Paulo paused. "Yes, this is New York." He drew deeply again on the cigarette. He had a serious look on his face. "Yes, this is New York…you're right, there are lots of different people here, but there is still family. My family. There's family and there's money." He paused again for a few moments. "It's impossible to be gay and be with my family. I'd be an outcast. That's why I go to the clubs, Michael. I like to have my own fun…real sex…but when it comes to serious matters like money, an Italian man has to have a wife and some children. Maybe it's an Italian thing, but deep down I don't think so. I think it's a man thing." Michael was surprised at how seriously Paulo had reacted to his question. His anger appeared to be building up, anger at the veil of secrecy around his own sexuality. "My father and my mother would never accept me being homosexual. End of story. I wouldn't want to hurt them. They tell me to marry this girl who is from a good Italian family, and I will marry." Paulo looked at Michael tenderly. "But it will not change how I feel about you, Michael. I think I have fallen in love with you…really. Usually it's just sex, but you're different." Paulo held Michael's hand and finished with, "It's different this time."

Michael lay there for nearly another ten minutes, finally making his excuses to Paulo. "I said I'd help Ernie out today and do another shift in the sex shop this afternoon so I'll have to leave.".

"You're too kind, sorry you can't stay longer" Paulo looked disappointed. Michael went to the bathroom, dressed quickly, and assured Paulo that he would meet him in the club that night. After an exchange of kisses Michael was out of the apartment. As he travelled down in the elevator, he was lost in his own world, turning around in his mind what Paulo had said. A nasty surprise greeted him when the doors opened on the ground floor: at the front doorway stood the menacing figure of Stefano with two other men who were in deep conversation with the doorman. He didn't want Stefano to see him and start asking awkward questions, so he took a right turn towards the stairs, continuing down to the basement and making his escape onto street level at the back of the building. His mind was racing. What was Stefano doing there? Instinctively, he felt it had something to do with Paulo. Deep down he was beginning to feel that his lover was trouble – trouble with a large T.

MICHAEL CLOSED the library book as the train pulled into the subway station. He was doing another shift at "Secret Delights" for Ernie, who was still suffering from a racking cough despite a few courses of antibiotics. The afternoon shift finished in the early evening, when he would head to his own job in the restaurant. Michael found the sex shop highly amusing, especially when some of the regular lunchtime customers crept in sheepishly, trying hard not to make eye contact with whoever was behind the counter. If the shop was quiet, he read the library books he had got on Pearl's ticket, today's books being a history of footwear and a book on China with a chapter on binding women's feet. Since the night of the fashion show, he had become more and more fascinated by shoes. He was now absolutely certain he wanted to do something, anything, in the shoe fashion industry.

At the back of the shop was a small stage where a girl danced semi-naked, watched by men who squeezed themselves into dimly lit booths, each of which had a single chair, a box of tissues and a coin slot that the punters fed to open a shutter to give them a view of the action. All the dancing girls had perfected the moans and groans almost like a song as they danced away while their minds were elsewhere. Within a few minutes the timed spring would pop to close the shutter, blocking the view of the stage and leaving the punter with the option of leaving if they didn't want to just sit in the dark or inserting more money.

One of the dancers was already at the shop when Michael arrived.

"Hello, Monica, how's it going?" Michael smiled warmly as he was greeted by a beautiful young woman who let him into the darkened shop.

"Hi there, Michael, are you filling in for Ernie again?" Monica's welcoming smile showed off dazzlingly perfect American teeth. "Fresh coffee made out the back, help yourself. We don't have to open up for another twenty minutes."

"Yea, I'm filling in for Ernie again. He's got another doctor's appointment. I don't mind really, it gives me time to catch up on my reading."

Michael followed Monica to the kitchen. He could hear banging and hammering from the builders who were making an extension to the shop at the back. "Are those tasty Irish builders still feasting their eyes on your beautiful body at every opportunity?" Michael asked with a giggle.

He poured out two coffees and they sat at a small table. Monica was dressed in a fake fur coat that covered most of her tiny body, her small feet peeping out of the bottom and showing ankle socks and woollen slippers. She smiled as she opened the coat to reveal red silk underwear held together with a tight suspender belt.

"When I introduced myself to the builders as 'Wet Wanton Wendy' you could see the blood draining from their faces and going straight to other parts of their bodies." Monica had a type of humour that Michael loved. "Then I explained that 'Sucking Sandy' was on her day off today and it was my shift. Well it was all too much information at once, so I left them and ran in here to the kitchen."

What amused Michael especially was the fact that Monica was not interested in men but lived with her girlfriend Kirsten in Brooklyn. They were both studying for law degrees and 'Wet Wanton Wendy's' wages went a long way towards paying their college fees.

"What are the builders doing to the shop anyway?" Michael asked. "Won't all that banging and hammering put off the regular lunchtime trade?"

"I'll just turn up the music a bit louder. I don't think it will affect business. It's only the older, regular guys who come in around lunchtime. Most of them are a bit deaf anyway." Monica got up to leave. "They're adding more of the small private booths, Michael, just like the ones we have already, but they are putting in another six. The boss says they make the most money in the whole shop. A dollar a minute, Michael, imagine a dollar a minute to watch me in my panties, hear me moaning and groaning as I pretend to play with myself. It's very funny really. If only the dirty old men knew that most times I'm just lying there either thinking about my shopping list or what I'll do with my girlfriend when I get home. Men, their brains are in their pants." She stopped when she realised what she said. "Well, present company excluded, of course."

"Of course," Michael said, not taking offence. "Off you go, Monica, do your thing and I'll open the shop."

"Just one thing, c'mon, I want to show you. Bert, the regular rubber doll guy, his latest blow-up is in."

They moved towards the order drawer and she took out a package that had come in from China the previous day. "It has these extra large openings in the shape of ruby red lips, both top and bottom of the doll. One opening at the mouth and one right in between the doll's long legs. It says guaranteed suction."

Michael was amazed when he began to read the description on the package.

"Yeah, you're right, Monica…it says guaranteed suction. Guess old Bert is sure of a good tight kiss tonight, but maybe not on his face!'

"Guess you're right there." Monica tittered and laughed. "Isn't it kinda strange, Michael, these men look so normal when they come into the shop and then they go home to their wives. Yuck."

"Exactly like the type of men I used to see every Sunday when I'd go to Mass back in Ireland."

"Yeah, weird, right, and then they say it's wrong to be gay. You know, by the time I finish working here in this shop, I reckon I should get a degree in psychology because most people are a bit crazy. There is no such thing as normal." She made her way towards the back of the shop.

"You've got it right there, Monica. Now put on your dancing face and go for it. I'll stock the shelves and we'll have more coffee in an hour or two." Michael turned on the sign on the front door and hit the lights; the shop was ready for business.

Michael was becoming more used to the shop's merchandise, such as the different shaped objects for insertion into the human body, some battery-operated and some manual. There were add-ons and extra extension bits, all coming in their own different colours. At first his mind had boggled at what he saw, but now it seemed like stacking candy on the shelves, just a more grown-up form of candy. Sometimes he would flick through the books and magazines as he arranged them. Some of the women appeared to have bendy, flexible legs which never met together, and all had extra-large breasts. Most of them looked like clones to him, every single one of them the same.

Michael sat peacefully reading his books as the regular customers came and went. One of them was a guy about the same age as Michael, his face and neck covered in acne. He looked dirty and greasy and seemed to have the same clothes every time he was in the shop. The fifty-dollar bill he used to pay for his usual purchase of a large stack of books and magazines confirmed to Michael that he wasn't homeless, just a bit of a pervert. Michael never made eye contact but just wrapped up the magazines in the mandatory plain brown paper bag. After a while Bert, the regular rubber doll customer, came in to collect "Large Lips Lucy". He looked nearly seventy, Michael thought, as Bert smiled at him.

"I forgot my reading glasses, son, could you just make sure it's the right one and read the label for me." Michael read out the details from the package. As soon as Bert heard Michael's accent he launched into a rambling account about himself and his family connections with 'little old Ireland'. Bert had been there many times to find his ancestral roots, and loved Ireland. He took out some photographs of his grand-kids from his wallet to show them to Michael.

"You're all such friendly people, you Irish. I even managed to kiss the Blarney Stone when I was there," was Bert's parting line as he gathered up 'Large Lips Lucy'. Michael found it hard to look Bert in the eye in case he would burst out laughing. As Bert had been rambling on about his love of Ireland, all Michael could think about was an image of Bert holding the blown-up version of the rubber doll. Which extra large opening would he use first? He shuddered at his own thoughts, smiling as Bert left the shop.

Other customers arrived. Even one of the builder's friends, Micko, a big horse of a man from Mayo, came in and pretended that he was going to help the other builders with the extension but as he headed to the back began to check out the merchandise. Michael watched him from the corner of his eye. He was sure that Micko was getting excited. His funny walk indicated that something was happening in his pants. Michael smiled to himself, ignoring it all; he had much more interest in his books.

Suddenly there was an unmerciful crash, a bang, and a sudden pause, followed by high-pitched screams from the back of the shop. Michael and Micko ran towards the noise. When they got there they could see the wooden booths had all collapsed to the ground, while Monica lay in a state of shock on the stage, dressed only in her panties. There had only been two customers in the booths, one of them an old man with a stick, who always came into the shop on a Wednesday. He had fallen asleep sitting on the chair in the small booth; his trousers were on the floor around his ankles. He wasn't moving, so two of the builders rushed to see if he was alive or dead. He woke up with a jolt from the force with which they shook his shoulders and looked around with a dazed look on his face. As soon as they had helped him to pull up his long johns and trousers, he grabbed his walking stick and with a few dissatisfied grunts limped out of the shop.

The second man in the booths was a regular lunchtime client, a man in his mid-forties, who, with his Armani suit and hand-made shoes, looked like someone who was well off. Right now, he stood with his designer trousers and underpants down around his ankles. Michael was sure the man was about to have a heart attack because his face was so flushed with embarrassment. He stood almost as if in a trance, and everyone in the room stood in silence staring at him as the music continued to play. Then Michael saw the enlarged protruding part of his body which he held tightly with his right hand. After a number of seconds the man suddenly realised what had happened. Michael had never seen a man move as fast, just like an Olympic runner first off the block, as he pulled up his underpants and his trousers, and then grab his briefcase, almost in one sweeping movement, before sprinting past them and out the front door.

Monica, Michael and the builders allowed themselves to start laughing loudly. One of the builders bent down and picked up a card from the floor. "It's your man's card," he announced with a loud titter in his voice. "He's an investment banker on Wall Street, says here no investment is too big or too small for him to handle."

Monica piped in: "Wonder does he wash his hands first?" She looked around at the others before delivering her punchline: "I mean, before he handles your investments." More raucous laughter filled the shop and then rose again when Micko added: "He looked like he could fairly handle his own investments – judging by the tight grip he had on them today."

As he headed towards the restaurant at five that evening, Michael stopped to buy a postcard, writing a message to Padraig and then popping in the mailbox.

DUNGLASS, IRELAND 1986

"WHAT DO you call this, young lady?" Siobhan's father handed her the postcard from Michael. Siobhan looked at the image of a bikini clad young woman in a body-builder pose who pumped out her bulging veins and muscular body.

"No need to panic, Dad. It's just a bit of a joke between myself and Michael." They were sitting in the kitchen about to eat their dinner together. Siobhan lived alone with her dad, while her two married brothers lived in Dublin. As the local Garda sergeant and, in his own eyes, a pillar of the community, Patrick Daly felt that high moral standards had to be adhered to at all times, especially in his own home. He glared at his daughter. "That's not a very nice thing for a young lady like you to get in the post. Mrs Fitzpatrick at the Post Office must have read it. Imagine what she is thinking"

"Don't be over-reacting. Dad, it's only a card. Have your dinner and let's watch the television as usual."

Siobhan's mother had died at forty-eight from cancer five years previously, leaving a cold, cheerless house. The hardest part was living with her dad's constant fear of "what the neighbours would say." Siobhan and her father were worlds apart, such different types of people. While Siobhan had great flair and imagination her father was compliant to rules and regulations beyond belief.

They were eating their dinner in the usual silence when out of the blue he said, "I know the matron in Portrane, the psychiatric hospital. I got you the form, you fill it out and I can get you in."

"As what, Dad? A patient?" She often enjoyed antagonising him.

"Don't take that tone with me, Siobhan. I meant as a student nurse of course. It's time you got yourself a proper job, no more of this working in Woolworth's. We didn't bring you this far, myself and your mother, to have you working just as a shop girl."

"I happen to like working just as a shop girl, Dad, as you put it. I actually like it there, so why would I want to work in a psychiatric hospital?"

"You have the build for a good nurse – for lifting those patients. All that boxing you did at school would help. You've a fine pair of shoulders on you, girl. They're taking on student nurses in October. In three years you'd be qualified."

"I don't want to be a psychiatric nurse, Dad. Does that not occur to you?"

"We all have to do things in life we don't want to at times. You should be thinking of the future." His policeman's voice was coming through. "Getting yourself a man, getting married and having a couple of kids, like your brothers."

"What if I didn't want that, Dad? What if I was different, what if I was gay? How would you feel about that?" Siobhan had said it without thinking.

He gave a dismissive grunt. "All this modern talk about being

45

gay, I read it in the paper every day, all these people coming out of the closet, such rubbish. It isn't right this gay talk, and it's not what God intended."

Siobhan played around with her food as she watched her father finish off every morsel on his plate. A sickening feeling hit her stomach. She realised she would never fit in here in this house or in Dunglass. Although they both had the same blood running through their veins, they were from different planets. He just didn't understand her and he never would.

"But Dad, there are different types of people in the world. Not everyone wants a steady, pensionable job."

"Look, girl, that's enough. As I've said, no more of this talk of gay in my house. Young people…you've got too much, that's all that's wrong with you. When I was a young fellow in Mayo, we had an outside toilet for ten of us, we walked five miles a day to school, helped my father in the fields every day after school, and it did us no harm. You fill out that form now and you'll get yourself a job in that hospital." The conversation was over as far as he was concerned.

Siobhan made the usual pot of tea, buttered some currant bread and left it with a pot of jam in front of him. She would have to escape, but wasn't yet sure how or when. One thing was certain, she wasn't going to spend the rest of her life doing what her father wanted, to make him happy and the envy of his neighbours. Psychiatric nurse? "I've probably earned a degree in nutters having to deal with you over the last few years," she said to herself Hadn't he made life a hell for her poor mother? But that was not somewhere she wanted to go right now. She cleared away the table and made a start on the washing-up.

IT HAD been a rough day in the salon. Padraig let himself in

46

the front door of the house feeling exhausted. The second post-card had arrived that morning from Michael in New York about working in the sex shop.

Hi Padraig, Worked in a sex shop today. It was 'Sucking Sandy's day off, so 'Wet Wanton Wendy' did live dance shift instead! Teased all old men, to point of no return!! Best laugh is: she's a lesbian!! Have applied to a fashion college in London and hope to hear from them soon. If I get in, maybe you will come with me. Fill you in when I get home. You go easy on your old biddy customers with their blue rinses. Wish you were here. Michael x

Padraig had a laugh when he read it but felt a bit depressed all day in the salon when he looked around at the people he was dealing with. He was in bad humour when he got home. He found his father Seamus in the sitting room, glued as usual to the television, It was early evening and the house was empty.

"Well, Padraig, how are you?"

"Huh" was all Padraig could manage to mumble, feeling resentful and angry. Not sure at what or whom but maybe at everything and everybody. This godforsaken small town, the godforsaken job he had. "Yeah, I'm fine, Dad. Got a postcard today from Michael, would you like to read it?" He handed him the postcard. His father put his glasses on and read it, and read it again

Sucking Sandy's day off, so 'Wet Wanton Wendy' did live dance shift.

"That's some place that boy is working in, and he's supposed to be a friend of yours. Respectable mother and father and all, it's a disgrace."

"What do you mean it's a disgrace? There's a big world out there, Dad, not everyone is like you…marrying someone for their money." Padraig wanted to hurt his father as much as he could.

Seamus Flood was a widower with two children and had married Bridie, a wealthy businesswoman with one daughter. The idea of having a rich step-mother had appealed to Padraig and his sister Martha, but while Bridie might have liked their dad she resented his children and had made their lives hell since they had all moved into her house on the posh side of town.

"Don't you ever talk about my wife like that again. Bridie has been a good mother to you. I won't have you say anything about her." Seamus stood up and the two stood staring into each other's face.

"Oh right, you won't have us say a bad word about her but its okay for her to treat us like dirt, me and Martha?" All the hurt and pain was bubbling up and had to come out. "It's okay for her to swan off to Spain with her daughter for a week, but never bring me or my sister on holiday? C'mon, Dad, face it, she has made us feel inferior from the very day she married you. The sooner I can get away from her and this house the better."

"Well there's no one chaining you here, away with you."

"Actually, I'm thinking about going to London. Michael's coming home soon and I'm going with him."

"Don't let me hold you back," Seamus sneered.

"Oh, and while we're at it, I just want you to know that I'm gay, homosexual, a fag, a queer. Padraig shouted out the words, knowing that each would be like a spear through his father's side. Seamus stood with his mouth open, the blood draining from his face.

"You're a disgrace to the family," Seamus said in shock.

"Just like you then, Dad. You're just a weak wimp of a man, always have been, so don't talk to me about bringing disgrace on the family." Seamus raised his right hand. Padraig stood staring into his eyes. "You go ahead," he said slowly. "Hit me, but just remember that I will hit you back." With his fist still raised and

48

clenched, Seamus glared silently at his son for a few seconds before dropping his hand back down by his side. Padraig looked straight ahead at his dad. All the anger he felt was now beginning to melt away. He turned on his heels and left the house quickly, slamming the front door as hard as he could. He cried as he walked through the spitting soft rain, his face partially covered with the hood of his jacket. He felt confused and hurt, but at least he had said what he had wanted to say for so long. He had opened a Pandora's Box of feelings and wasn't sure how to handle it. He had never felt so alone in his life.

"I GOT this amazing postcard from my friend today, Pearse." Cormac ventured. "It's of Grand Central train station in New York, it looks amazing." He looked over to Pearse who was lounging beside him on the bed. He knew Pearse didn't like conversation after sex but was beginning to wonder if he liked conversation at all. They usually met up every few nights at the graveyard when Pearse would drive to isolated country lanes or, like tonight, to his brother's mobile home in Faunstown. Pearse was his first real lover. Fumbles and kisses with other guys at the back of the sheds at school or quickie offers from horny husbands on holiday with their wives and kids at the holiday camp made up Cormac's sexual history to date. His drunken encounters with girls at discos had always felt like kissing a cardboard box. He was amazed at how he reacted when he was with Pearse; just the feel or smell of his skin made him melt, and every cell in his body tingled and came alive when he touched him. The explosive, wild release that followed each time only made Cormac want more. Yet it was starting to dawn on him that the only two things Pearse ever spoke about was how his girlfriend Jackie was getting on his nerves (which Cormac always liked to hear) or about a horse he had backed that day and how he couldn't wait for his annual trip to Cheltenham.

"Had another floater today in the pool," Cormac said, thinking he'd try a bit of comedy to delay their departure. Pearse was already out of the bed getting dressed.

"What do you mean, floater?" he said with a look of indifference on his face.

"One of the kids did a big pooh in the swimming pool, and as usual, it floated to the top," Cormac said laughing, "and of course, guess who had to clean it up? God I hate kids." Pearse did a kind of sniggering sound and pretended to listen. "Guess its time to go back then," Cormac said disappointedly.

"Look, I'm sorry, Cormac, I know it's been short this time but sometime soon we'll have more time, honestly." Pearse found himself apologising but he was anxious to get back to Dunglass for closing time. They left the mobile home and as Pearse locked the door behind them, Cormac stood gazing up at stars in the clear black night. "There are millions and millions of them, Pearse. Have you ever read anything about the stars?"

"I've never read a book in my life," Pearse replied, turning up the taxi radio loud to indicate it was the end of the conversation. Cormac tried again.

"My friend tells me there is a new gay bar in Dublin. What do you say we hit Dublin some night, maybe we could even stay over?" For a split second Pearse allowed the car to veer to the left in shock at the thought of them being seen together, but managed to gain control as he mumbled a reply.

"Yeah, I'll think about it, leave it with me. I've no money at the moment, lost a few bob at the weekend on the horses, and the saving for the deposit on the house, but sometime we will." In an instant he put his foot down on the accelerator; it was clear to Cormac that he wanted to get him to the drop-off point as quickly as possible.

Cormac was overwhelmed by loneliness as he stood outside the graveyard and watched the taxi speed off. He had read letters in his mother's weekly magazine about women feeling let down and used. He now knew that men could feel the same.

PADRAIG CHECKED his watch for the umpteenth time as he sat at the kitchen table. He had ten minutes to munch a quick breakfast of buttered toast before he was due to meet Siobhan. His mind was buzzing with excitement at the thought of the day ahead in Dublin. They'd catch the bus and be in O'Connell Street in less than an hour. Siobhan had plans to buy the latest sports gear while Padraig's mind was more on the lingerie departments in the large stores.

"Where's your dad?" Bridie called as she walked through the kitchen door, jolting Padraig into defence mode.

"What? Am I his keeper?" Padraig snapped automatically. Bad start, his mind told him, but every time he saw his stepmother something inside him ignited.

"A day off then, Padraig, what are your plans?" Bridie continued as she made herself a cup of coffee, making sure to avoid eye contact with him. "Suppose you're hitting the shops in Dublin again?"

"I thought of getting red knickers today and maybe a red wig to go with them." Padraig's bitterness was apparent in his tone. He knew that Bridie rummaged through the stuff in his room at every opportunity and had come across his collection of ladies' underwear. He disliked this fat woman intensely and could never understand why his father had married her so quickly after his mother's death.

Taking her coffee and heading towards the sitting room, Bridie knew the moment had come to press the right button.

"Imagine what your poor mother would have said." Bridie stalled, waiting to see how her poison would work. "Transvestite, I suppose they call it?" Padraig's whole body stiffened, waiting for the final blow. "Abnormal or damaged is what I call it." Bridie's lingering eyes brightened at the impact of her remarks.

The sound of the front door opening signalled his dad's return from the shop with the newspapers. Bridie's tone sweetened immediately as she greeted him, making Padraig's stomach churn even more as he pushed away his uneaten toast. He grabbed his hold-all and coat and headed for the front door but then turned around to stare straight at Bridie.

"I'll check for you if they have those knickers in your size," he said slowly. "Extra, extra large in the fat ladies' section." Slamming the door hard behind him, Padraig grinned from ear to ear as he broke into a run to the bus stop where Siobhan would be waiting.

On their way to Dublin Padraig told Siobhan his latest news: he had enrolled in an evening class in the city and was learning to become a make-up artist. "I love it, Siobhan, it gives us all these great tips about make up, amazing the difference it can make when applied properly." The students were all women except him and another young gay man called George, with whom he had become quite friendly. "George has asked me to help him do this gig Friday night," he added.

"Sounds intriguing, what kind of a gig?" Siobhan asked.

"George goes to people's houses. They invite their friends and he does a makeover." Padraig paused. "The only difference with Friday night is it's all men." Padraig emphasised the last word by raising his eyebrows.

"Wow," Siobhan said, her eyebrows also lifting. "Should be interesting."

"That's what I thought, so anyway I'm going along to help him out. Don't know whether he wants me to dress up in any of

52

my gear or just help him with the make-up. Quite looking forward to it," Padraig giggled.

After each had done their bits of shopping in the city they hooked up again outside Brown Thomas on Grafton Street and made their way to Lily's, a gay bar just a few streets away. It was small and dimly lit, with a mixture of young people who either looked like students or businessmen in suits. Padraig tried hard not to stare at two men at the end of the bar with their arms around each other; open affection between two members of the same sex was uncommon even in Dublin. Siobhan ordered two pints of cider and they found two free stools in the middle of the bar.

"Don't look now," Siobhan whispered as she leaned her head down towards Padraig's face. Padraig immediately looked behind him and caught sight of Desmond whom he had met the last time they had been here. "I told you not to look," Siobhan snarled.

"Relax Siobhan, I'll be back shortly, shouldn't be too long." Padraig winked at Siobhan, patted her arm fondly and grinned at her as he walked to the other end of the bar. He whispered something in Desmond's ear and Siobhan watched as they both headed for the toilets. After about ten minutes Padraig came back, took his seat beside Siobhan and ordered two more pints of cider. Siobhan knew from the huge smile on his face and glow about his eyes that he had got some action.

"He sends you his blessing," Padraig whispered from the side of his mouth.

"Who sends his blessing?"

"Father Desmond," Padraig whispered back. Siobhan's mouth dropped open, but no words would come. After gathering herself she said:, "So there was conversation this time?"

On the bus back to Dunglass that evening they giggled and laughed about what had happened. "Answer me something, Siobhan." Padraig felt a little high from his encounter and the pints of cider. "If I've had sex with a priest in the toilets of a gay bar, does that mean I'm a nymphomaniac?"

"The only thing it means, Padraig, is you got lucky." Siobhan's voice was full of admiration and envy.

The bus moved on and they sat contentedly in silence when out of the blue Siobhan said: "Did I tell you Mary Rose has a new Garda boyfriend? He's one of the recruits, straight out of Garda college. You know she's a Garda-stalker, don't you?"

Padraig nodded. "Good pensionable job, wages every month for the rest of her life, boring, boring, boring. Well this one is a complete mulch head from the west of Ireland. You'd think he never saw a woman in his life before, but seemingly she played her nipple trick on him and it worked 'cos they're going out together three weeks and he's mad about her."

"What's the nipple trick?"

"It's where she goes to the toilets, pinches her nipples and they become erect, ready for action. She then prances out before the fellow she fancies, and with your man, Mr Mulch Head, it worked because he saw what was on offer, and now they're going out."

"Mission accomplished," Padraig threw in.

"Poor Finnuala, how is she doing?" he asked. "Now she's a different kettle of fish." He liked Finnuala. "Heard she got a job in the civil service, in the tax office, starting early October." Padraig got all his news in the salon, was the hive of information in Dunglass. "I know she still really likes Michael, but he should come clean and tell her straight out that he's gay. It's not fair on her."

"Well, unless he swings both ways," Siobhan said with a giggle.

"I'm too tired to think, I need a kip." Padraig closed his eyes and snuggled into Siobhan's left shoulder. Together they dozed as the bus left the bright lights of Dublin behind and headed towards Dunglass.

"YOU'RE WANTED on the phone, Cormac," his mother called. "It's someone from the holiday camp, I think." The phone had only been installed a short while so Cormac felt surprised that anyone would be calling him as he picked up the receiver.

"I need to see you, Cormac, meet me at the church in ten minutes." It was Pearse.

"Yes, that will be fine," Cormac said in a very official voice. Looking over his shoulder, he could see his mother was hovering in the sitting room trying to hear what was been said on the phone. After he finished the call he put his heavy jacket on, and his mother was out in a flash.

"Who was that, Cormac?"

"It was my manager from work mother. I have to do a few more shifts at the weekend. Listen, I'm heading over to Siobhan's, need to have a chat with her. Talk to you later, Mam."

When the taxi pulled up Cormac jumped into the front and Pearse sped off in the direction of one of their many country lane hideouts. Cormac could immediately sense something was wrong with Pearse. His death's grip with both hands on the steering wheel and the heavy sighs and tension oozing out of him put Cormac on edge. After a few miles Cormac started to chatter nervously about the postcard from Michael.

"Stop…enough…shut up," Pearse shouted. Cormac felt afraid that Pearse might hit him and so his shoulders shrank into the seat. When they finally arrived at a quiet, deserted spot Pearse's hands were shaking as he turned off the ignition and the radio. Cormac reached out to him

"What's wrong, Pearse? Something is wrong, tell me." For a long moment they sat in silence and Cormac could feel his heart pounding in his chest. At last Pearse spoke.

"She's pregnant"

"Who's pregnant?" Cormac asked innocently.

"Jackie, my girlfriend, Cormac, she's up the duff, stuffed, whatever word you want to call it." Pearse spat out the words.

Cormac immediately dropped Pearse's hands. "I thought you said you didn't have sex with her." Pearse stared straight ahead into the darkness.

"She says we have to get married. I don't want to get married." Pearse paused. "But she insists. It will be a rush job, a shotgun wedding. She wants to make it all legal before the baby comes. She says I have to stand by her."

Cormac couldn't take in the words; it was as if someone was hitting him in his stomach. They sat in silence, Cormac staring at Pearse, his mind racing. Did he talk too much? Did he bore him about postcards and films? What was wrong with him? Why was he so stupid to think he was having a real relationship with Pearse? Pearse continued to stare ahead.

"She said it was the day I got the big winner, when I backed a treble and won three hundred pounds. Went to McBride's and had a good few whiskies and too many pints. Didn't pull out in time, I can't remember that bit. She has it all down to the day, she has it all arranged. We're going to move in to her aunt's flat over the hairdressers down town. She has it all worked out. I don't want to be a father, don't want to get married, I don't know what to do." Suddenly he started to cry, throwing himself against Cormac's shoulder.

"These few months have been great. I still want to be with you, nothing has changed. We'll just lay off for a little while, just until the wedding is over, but I still want to see you. I don't want things to change between us, Cormac." Cormac held Pearse in his arms and stroked his hair and comforted him like he would a child. When he was all cried out Pearse drew away, dried his nose with his sleeve and wiped his face clear of tears. In the silence of the car at that moment Cormac made the decision: he would

56

go to London with Michael. He couldn't possibly hang around Dunglass and watch Pearse get married and play happy families. He felt very naïve and silly to have trusted and fallen in love with the man sitting beside him.

"Have we time for a quickie, do you think?" Pearse asked, looking directly at Cormac.

"I'd like to go home," Cormac said. He was afraid he would start to cry but managed to hold it together and firmly added, "Now."

The journey back was made in silence. Cormac was baffled. How could this brute of a man be soft and sensitive, crying like a baby one moment and then talk about a quickie in the next?

When he got out of the car Cormac walked deep in thought towards his house. Pearse, in the most unexpected of ways, had given him the push he needed, and in his mind a plan was starting to form.

NEW YORK, 1986

MICHAEL WAS sipping coffee with Pearl in her apartment and talking about his favourite topic, London. He was delighted when Pearl told him that she had applied to get into a creative writing course there. "I'm sure you'll get a place Pearl, especially when they see how good you are from your articles. London, think of it, and we can be there for one another."

"You're starting to sound very American, Michael. 'Be there for one another', so over-emotional." They laughed together. "What are your plans today?" Pearl asked. "More second-hand shops, I suppose? Honestly, Michael, don't the people in those shops think you're a bit crazy, sketching all those bags and shoes?"

"I don't know at this stage. I used to think about buying the

57

shoes but then they really would think I was crazy, me buying women's shoes and also I don't have room for them in the apartment. Some day I'll have my own studio and I can store all the shoes I want to help me with my ideas."

Michael was cramming in as much as possible in the time he had left in New York, visiting as many shops as he could in the afternoons before his shift at the restaurant. Glam Ernie had entertained his new boyfriend overnight, so Michael had come up to Pearl's apartment to give them time to have breakfast alone together. The thin walls of Ernie's apartment had meant that Michael was almost part of their bedroom antics, and even his earplugs couldn't block out the night's grunts and groans.

"I think I'll head off shortly myself, Pearl. I'm going to call to Fausto."

"Anything wrong there, you look a bit worried about him?"

"He looks older all of a sudden. His limp is more pronounced and he's just a bit all over the place. That's what I thought the last time I called. Might see you later."

A little while later, after coming out of the subway he walked towards Fausto's but could see as he got near that it was closed and in darkness. Peering through the window he managed to make out the figure of the old man in the gloom, slumped on a chair at the back of the shop. He knocked hard on the window a couple of times until Fausto woke up and then slowly walked towards the front door, opening it a fraction.

"Please, Michael, not today…today is not good. I close early… please, maybe you come back some other time." Fausto's speech was slurred and his breath smelled of alcohol. The old man hadn't shaved; his hair and clothing were very dishevelled.

"What's wrong, Fausto? Let me in, just for a quick chat." The old man swayed, unsteady on his feet, opened the door and then quickly locked it behind them. He walked slowly, dragging his leg towards the chair and collapsed back onto it.

"Pour me another whiskey," he said, pointing towards a half-empty bottle on the shelf. The shop looked as if it had been burgled with the chair overturned, magazines scattered all over the floor, and there was an eerie feeling about the place.

"Maybe we should go upstairs and I'll make you some coffee. C'mon, let's go up. I'll help you, maybe you should sleep for a while."

"Pour me a drink. Please Michael, do as I ask. Then we'll go upstairs." Michael filled the glass half full of whisky and handed it to the old man who sipped it as he stared ahead in silence. Michael sat beside him on a small stool and waited.

When he finished the whiskey they went up to he apartment overhead, which was small, neat and tidy, just like the old barber himself normally was. Fausto sat in his armchair, and Michael covered his knees with a blanket and took off his shoes for him. He made some strong coffee and watched the old man's hands shake as he drank it reluctantly.

"I'm finished...it's over," Fausto suddenly said. Michael said nothing at first, letting him slowly finish his coffee, but then gently asked what had happened.

"He comes for his money like he always does on a Friday. But now he wants more, he says he wants more money. It's not enough what I give him for the last twenty years but now he wants double on a Friday and I do not have it. I do not know what I will do Michael. I'm tired. My business is small and they are big people, the Lombardi family." Fausto paused. "They are owners of this area. Stefano comes...he threatens, and now he tells me I must give him double."

Michael began to feel his stomach churn sickeningly.

"The worse part, Michael," Fausto continued almost in a whisper, "when I was younger in my good days I tried to stand up

and fight, I refused to pay, and look, they took away my kneecap."
Fausto pointed to his right knee. "See my limp. It is why I find
it hard now to walk and to dance, but that was many years ago.
Now I just give them the money, I am too old to fight."

Fausto paused to point to an envelope on the shelf over the
small electric fire."Look there. Bring it to me." Michael took the
small white envelope back to Fausto, who emptied its contents
into the palm of his hand. There were two bullets. "He tells me
he wants double the money every Friday . . ." He paused to control the trembling in his voice. "Or bullets like these will go to my
grandchildren. He says he knows where they live."

Michael's suspicions that Stefano called regularly for protection
money were now confirmed. A shiver ran down his spine. He felt
helpless as he looked at the old man who seemed to have aged
and shrunk overnight.

"I say to you, Michael, you are young, you should go away
from here. Away from the Lombardi family, go home, Michael.
Go back to Ireland or some other place. Do not work for these
people, they are dangerous, very dangerous."

"What about the police, why do you not go there. Can they
not help?"

"No police…these people have the police in their pockets.
They pay them big money." Fausto's voice was distressed. "So no
police, Michael, please. I'm tired now…I need to sleep…maybe
you help me to bed." Michael helped the old man from the chair
towards the bedroom at the back of the apartment. Fausto lay on
top of the small single bed, and Michael covered him in a blanket.

"I'll call to you tomorrow, you'll be okay. Don't drink anymore
and we will think of something."

"You good boy, Michael. Go now, I see you again. Keep this
to yourself, Michael. I tired now…I sleep."

Fausto was asleep before Michael got to the bedroom door.

Letting himself out of the shop he made sure the front door was locked tightly behind him. On his way to the restaurant he called at a small cafe where he sat in a corner nursing a double espresso as he thought about everything Fausto had said. He felt dismayed, but he knew there was nothing he could do. The whole thing had rattled him; as soon as he got to the restaurant he would calm his nerves with a good stiff drink.

THE SOUND of Pavarotti singing hit Michael's ears as he entered the kitchen through the alleyway at the back of the restaurant. He immediately sensed something was different. Fat Maria was busy tucking in to leftovers from plates just back from the tables, which was unusual, as normally the restaurant didn't open until the evening.

"Was there something on today, Maria?" Michael asked as he headed to the staff room to change into his work shirt. Maria's mouth was full, but she managed to mumble, "Yeah, Michael, the engagement do is on today, it's one hell of a do…the wine is flowing like water. The whole family are there." Michael nodded, only half listening. His mind was still on Fausto, wondering if Ernie or Pearl would know what to do, or perhaps even Paulo. He returned from the staff room and, still distracted, asked Maria: "What do you want me to do first Maria? Where is Isabella?"

"Oh, Miss Isabella is right out in front, of course, wouldn't you know it?" There was a vicious tone to her voice. Michael was in no humour for getting involved so he just nodded. Maria continued, "Be on your best behaviour Michael and gather all the desserts, finish clearing up the plates. There is some amazing tiramisu out there and crème caramel. I look forward to tasting them." Michael straightened his clean apron and made his way out to the tables with a tray of clean glasses. The restaurant was full of designer-dressed people, all speaking Italian and most of them quite drunk. Others were dancing in a space cleared between the tables. Michael was gazing at the dancers when he was suddenly rooted to the spot with shock: standing in the middle of the room with their arms closely intertwined were Francesca Lombardi, the restaurant owner's daughter, and Paulo, looking like a golden couple from a magazine. Michael moved back into the darkness of a booth next to the kitchen so that Paulo would not see him. A waitress called Jackie was all smiles to Michael as she gathered up glasses.

"Isn't it marvellous, Michael? Look, aren't they so in love?"

"Was this some kind of party?" Michael asked innocently.

"It's their engagement party, Paulo and Francesca. Isn't she so beautiful? Her Valentino dress is stunning and I'd kill for those Gucci shoes. She looks like a young Sophia Loren."

Michael felt like someone had kicked him in his stomach. A feeling of dread gripped his chest and he was finding it hard to catch his breath. Was this the same Paulo who only the night before last had insisted he loved him and that they would work out how to be together? He had his suspicions about Paulo's protestations of love, and Paulo had mentioned a few times about getting married, but it was still a shock to see him with his arms around the spoilt heiress of a Mafia family. He turned to move towards the kitchen to get some air, when the room started to spin. Everyone looked in his direction as the tray of glasses came crashing down. Michael had fainted and was lying on the ground unconscious.

When he opened his eyes he wanted to jump up and run away with embarrassment, but his legs felt like jelly so he had to be helped to his feet by two other waiters who guided him towards the kitchen. The staff fussed over him as he sat in the kitchen. He felt ashamed and embarrassed, insisting he was fine; he would be okay in a moment, all he needed was some air.

"Give him a brandy, a large one," Isabella ordered.. A large brandy was placed in front of Michael which he lowered back in two mouthfuls.

"I'm fine Isabella, thank you. I'm fine, honestly. I'll be okay to do my shift in a moment." He still wondered, however, how he was going to get through this evening.

"You should go home," Isabella said. "Maybe you are not well. Go out to the alley to get some fresh air and I'll come in a few minutes with your wages."

"Ah, no," Michael said, "no…you're very kind."

"I insist," Isabella said. Michael walked unsteadily to the staff room to gather his belongings. On his way back to the kitchen, Paulo was waiting for him in the darkened corridor.

"I am so sorry, Michael."

"Get out of my way, Paulo. I don't feel so good. I'm waiting in the alley for Isabella to give me my wages and I'm going home. Just leave it at that."

"Please, let me explain. You don't understand, you're not Italian. It's only a cover-up, please, you must not let us be over." Paulo took out his leather Prada wallet and stuffed a five hundred dollar bill down the front of Michael's shirt.

"Please take this, buy something nice. I'll talk to you tomorrow…buy some nice thing for yourself…I am sorry." Michael stared straight into Paulo's face.

"Do you think I am some kind of male prostitute?" He spat the words as he pushed passed Paulo to the kitchen and headed for the alley. The cold, crisp air helped to bring him back to reality. Maria came out with another large brandy.

"Here, Michael, take this other one, it will help. Maybe you have a stomach bug. You eat some pasta when you go home, you'll be fine." He downed the brandy in one go and after Maria left he retrieved the five hundred dollar bill from the front of his shirt. As he stared at the money he wondered if he really was some kind of male prostitute. A part of him wanted to run back into the restaurant, to scream and shout at Paulo and throw his money back at him in front of everybody. But what would be the point? He shoved the money into his trouser pocket. Within a few minutes Isabella arrived with a brown envelope.

"This is tonight's wages, Michael. Come back tomorrow night and make sure you don't eat anything funny again.." She handed him a third large brandy which he gulped back. He felt dizzy as he began to walk towards the street at the front of the restaurant. He could see a figure in the semi-darkness near the top of the alley.

"Please, Michael . . ." Paulo went to hold Michael. "Please give me one hug, I need to hold you. I feel so bad. If we meet tomorrow I will explain everything." Michael felt unsteady on his feet and was unable to resist Paulo taking hold of his shoulders and placing his back against the wall. Paulo's left hand touched Michael's cheek as he said, "I love you, Michael, truly I love you. I want to be with you, please don't go anywhere. We can talk tomorrow." Michael felt numb from all that had happened but suddenly sobered slightly as he saw the huge figure of Stefano approaching.

"Take your hands off him," Stefano hissed "NOW." Instantly Paulo let go of Michael as if his hands had touched a red hot fire. Stefano, who was standing so close that Michael could smell his aftershave, stared at Paulo with vicious eyes

"Go back to your fiancée and to the family now," he spat. "This goes no further, get back now!" Michael stood rooted to the ground as he watched Paulo immediately button his jacket, rub his face with both hands and walk swiftly around the corner to the front door of the restaurant. The silence hung for a long moment as the two men stared at each other. Michael's ears instantly registered the sound of a flick-knife and then saw the glint of the knife Stefano held in his right hand. He moved it up close to Michael's face. Michael could feel the sharpness of the blade as it touched his cheek. With his left hand Stefano held Michael in a vice grip around his throat, making it hard for him to breathe.

"If I see you around here again I will cut your face into thin slices, peeling it off with my knife. It will look like spaghetti by the time I am finished. You understand?" Stefano's eyes flared wildly at Michael, who was unable to speak but nodded in agreement.

Stefano gave Michael one final menacing look, bringing the blade away from his cheek and moving it to eye level so he could get a full view of the knife. In an instant he turned away and walked right around to the front of the restaurant as if nothing had happened. Left alone in the darkened alley, Michael could feel liquid running down his legs, and he knew he had wet himself with fear. He wanted to get back to the apartment as quickly as possible. Taking a deep breath, he placed his jacket around the middle of his body, covering his legs and the stained pants and he ran from the alley as quick as he could towards the subway. He was glad it was dark, and no one took any notice of him.

He bought a large bottle of Jack Daniels and forty cigarettes at the local store and when he got to the apartment he was relieved it was empty. He stripped and showered and then made his way to a chair near the window, opening it to let the balmy heat of the summer evening come through. He chain-smoked and drank as much whisky as his stomach would hold. Eventually he staggered to his bedroom, threw himself on the bed and fell into a drunken sleep.

FOR A few seconds after Michael opened his eyes he wasn't sure quite where he was. The inside of his mouth was dry, as if his tongue had been replaced by a roll of sandpaper. A feeling of panic surged through his body but then subsided when he realised he was in his own small bed in Ernie's apartment. His hands shook as he swallowed two painkillers and gulped down a pint glass of water and refilled it. He dragged himself to the kitchen table, his legs as heavy as lead.

Images of Stefano's knife flashed in his mind as he went though everything that had happened at the restaurant. These thoughts were suddenly interrupted by the realisation that he had run to the bathroom several times during the night to vomit, but had done so in the bathtub and not the toilet. He would have to clean up the mess before Ernie got back.

As the painkillers kicked in and the pain eased he hauled himself from the kitchen table and headed to the bathroom to clean the bathtub but not before giving one final heave at the sight of his own vomit.

Back at the kitchen table he dragged slowly on a cigarette, thinking deeply about what he should do. There was only one option, he realised. The large hold-all under his bed would carry all his clothes, but his main concern was all the sketches and the designs he had done over the past weeks. They were all held in a slim briefcase he had picked up in one of the second-hand shops, and he would make sure this came on the plane with him as hand luggage.

An hour later Pearl knocked on the door to call for her daily coffee. Michael let her in with his head down, avoiding direct eye contact. "I've fresh doughnuts from Joey's bakery," she said as she went straight to the table. "Been up since seven o'clock, great to be alive. Oh my God, what happened to you, you look terrible, are you ill, Michael? Your face is the strangest colour I've ever seen."

"That's enough, Pearl," Michael managed to say sheepishly as he ran past her to the bathroom to vomit again. When he returned Pearl had two cups of coffee ready and was waiting for him at the table.

"C'mon, Michael, spill the beans. What happened last night?"

Michael sipped the coffee slowly and told her the events of the previous night. Speaking the words, relaying what had actually happened, made it more real to him, and he realised the trouble he was really in.

"What are you going to do, Michael? A knife…scary stuff." Pearl's voice was coming fast with shock.

"Scary? I thought my life was over, Pearl." Michael paused. "I really did. It was like my whole life flashing by in front of my eyes. You have no idea of the nightmares I've had all night. I'm going home today, Pearl, back to Ireland."

"But you can't, Michael. You're supposed to be here for another month. You can get a job in a different restaurant."

"No, I've made up my mind. I'm going to gather my stuff, head for JFK and get a standby ticket. I can change my ticket, it's a return. Whatever I have to do, I'll go and wait at the airport. I'm taking no chances. You should have seen the hate in Stefano's eyes, he meant business. As for Paulo, I feel stupid, naïve."

He started to sob like a child. Pearl moved over to him and held him in her arms as she let him cry it out.

When he was finished, she tried to make light of the situation. "Your face is a mess, Michael. Your eyes are swollen and red and you've a runny nose." She smiled as she went to the bathroom, returning with a damp facecloth, soap and some tissues. "C'mon, wash your face, blow your nose and we'll get you sorted for your journey."

Michael cleaned himself up and then went to his bedroom to pack his stuff. After, he and Pearl sat and chatted again until nearly lunch time when Glam Ernie arrived back, singing as he made his entrance.

"What's happening kids?" He looked from one to the other. "What's wrong? Have you two been to a funeral?"

"I'm sorry, Ernie, but I have to go home," Michael said. "I'm paid up for another month but I'm on my way out for the subway now in the next half hour. I was waiting to say goodbye to you."

Ernie sat at the kitchen table and listened as Michael relayed the story of Fausto, of what happened at the restaurant and Stefano's knife.

Ernie tried to make light of it all at first. "Oh my God, Michael, there's action and there's real action. You've had more excitement here in two months than I've had in five years." He then saw the look in Michael's eyes and became serious. "You're right. They are not a family to be messed with. So I think you're right to go home and stay clear. Lie low for a while. Come back again another time, but for the moment get away." He then began to cry, insisting that Michael keep in touch. Michael felt sad at leaving this larger-than-life friend.

On the way out of the building he instinctively checked the mail box. There were two letters for him, which he stuffed into his briefcase without giving them a glance.

Pearl insisted on going with Michael in the taxi to JFK and they linked each other affectionately as they sat in the back seat. At the Aer Lingus desk he was told that he could change his ticket and there was a flight available in four hours' time. They found a busy coffee shop near the departure gate and chose a quiet corner.

"We both know it's not the end of our friendship," Pearl said.

"I know that, Pearl. I'm still a bit all over the place, but of course we'll stay in touch." Pearl walked with Michael right to the departure gate.

For a few moments they stood there in an awkward silence. "Guess I'd better go, Michael," Pearl finally said. "It will be dark soon and I want to get home on the subway before it gets too late."

They held each other in a tight embrace for a long moment, and then Michael was gone through the departure gate. Wiping away her tears, Pearl turned and joined the flow of people running for the subway.

Michael closed his eyes as the plane took off and felt his hand touching his small leather bum-bag which held his passport, ticket and money. The small pocket at the front held Paulo's five hundred dollar bill. The money might give him some satisfaction, but he doubted it. The alcohol from the previous night had worn off, and now he felt the raw pain in his chest of rejection and anger, but mainly anger at his own naivety.

He knew his world was about to become small again as he headed home. He continued to brood for a while on the resentment he felt towards Paulo, but above all Stefano, until he remembered the two letters he had put hurriedly into his briefcase. Pulling them out, he saw one was clearly from his mother, with the address written in her familiar handwriting. The other was a typewritten envelope which he stared at in a daze, wondering what such an official looking letter had to do with him until he saw printed on its top left-hand corner the words, "London College of Fashion". He opened it slowly, gripped with a sense of dread that he was about to get more bad news. He had to read the contents twice before it sunk in and then allowed himself a silent whoop of joy.

The college had been very impressed by his designs and application letter and because of this, along with his results in the first year at the college of art, they would be glad to offer him a place in their shoe design course.

His world, he realised, was not going to shrink to the size of Dunglass for much longer.

"OH, THE dead arose," Michael's mother Alice said with a laugh as he entered the kitchen.

Michael had slept most of the time since returning home two days previously. He was jet-lagged and still confused and emotional after his quick exit from New York. Being back in a small cramped house in a council estate in small town made him feel he had arrived on a different planet.

"What time will Dad be home, Mam?" he asked.

"Be at least another hour before his duty finishes. He'll be finished for the weekend then." Michael's father was an army sergeant based at the barracks ten miles from Dunglass. The household reflected his regimental lifestyle; all had to be prim and proper and run like clockwork.

"Mam, I'd like to have a chat with you" Michael said. "Maybe we could have a cup of tea together?" He filled the kettle with water as he spoke. Alice was busy rolling fish in flour and placing it on a large plate to fry later.

"We're always talking, Michael, but go on, chat away there. I'll keep going here…lots to do. Rita will be in from work and James will be home from playing football. They'll all be home and will want their dinner on the table when they get in. What do you want to talk about?"

"After being in New York, Mam, for the last few months, I realise I want to specialise in designing shoes. Getting a place in the college in London is a real opportunity . . ." His mother cut across him.

"That shoe thing, Michael, again. There's another apprenticeship coming up in the army for an electrician, like last year, remember? Your dad can arrange an interview, no problem, and you know he could help you get the job. An apprenticeship is always good, there's always work for an electrician. Rita's Eugene is an electrician and they're able to save plenty of money to get married. There are always jobs to be done by electricians."

"Mam, we've been through this already. You know I don't want to be an electrician."

"Oh, I forgot . . . being a tradesman is not good enough for our Michael, he wants to be a shoe designer, an art student. I don't want another argument. The last time you messed up the interview your dad got for you."

Michael sat at the kitchen table and looked at his mother as he sipped his tea. Although only in her mid-forties she looked nearer sixty, a result of living with his dad's regime. Michael had never understood his dad. He provided well for his family, but showing affection was completely alien to him.

"Mam, can you sit down please, it will only take five minutes," he pleaded. Alice looked directly at him, and realised there was something serious he wanted to say. She sat down at the table and started to sip her cup of tea. "Mam, when I was in New York I kinda…things happened for me," Michael started to say, then paused, trying to think of the best way to tell his mother that he was homosexual without stabbing her with words. He treaded softly and continued gently. "New York is a big place with lots of different things, lots of different kinds of people. It's a big world and I realised that I'm not like anyone from around here in Dunglass. I'm not like the rest of the family but…I'm gay. Mam, I'm actually a gay man. . . I'm homosexual." He stopped speaking to let the words sit there and see how she was taking it. His mother put the cup down out of her hands as they started to tremble.

"Don't attempt to say that to your father," she said, and a few moments' silence fell between them.

"Mam, I've always known I was gay and I think you have too. You know I'm different, that's why I've decided I'm going to go to London. Then maybe I can live my life just for who I am, not stay here to do what my dad might want me to do, get an apprenticeship in the army, have a few kids. It would be wrong, I wouldn't be myself."

"But how do you know you're gay, Michael? I mean, lots of boys your age…they're young, they try different things…it doesn't mean anything. It just means you haven't yet decided. How can you be so sure? I mean…like…what's wrong with you? There's nothing wrong with Rita. She has a boyfriend and James is interested in girls. I mean, they are your brother and sister, so why can't you be like them?"

She paused momentarily for breath and then continued. "As well as that you know it's against God, it's against the Church. I mean, you'll be struck down dead, you'll go to hell, really Michael maybe you should think about it…if you stay around here you can't be gay…there's just no way…you'd have a horrible life here, you know. There are no gays in Ireland…maybe in America but we all know America is full of strange people and I mean it's so far away." Michael knew how his mother would rant when she became nervous about anything. He didn't interrupt but let her run out of steam until again a silence hung in the air between them. They each took a sip of their tea. Michael looked directly at his mother and he could feel the love coming from her. Alice put her hand on his.

"Listen Michael, I love you, you're my flesh and blood. I want you to remember that, but maybe it would be for the best that you go to London and stay there because really you can never say that to your father. It wouldn't be right, not in this house…so I'm sorry to say it but best you go to London or Dublin or back to New York. I'll say the prayer to St Jude, the saint for hopeless cases. Who knows? Maybe a nice girl will come along and things might be different, but for now Michael, I'd like you never ever to

mention that again. So look, I'm going to get the dinner here...
it's time those chips were on, so you set the table, be a good boy."
Alice rose from the table, the sign that the conversation was over.

Michael sat for another moment, disappointment, exhaustion
and jet-lag running through him. He had known how it would
go, but he had hoped that with his absence over the summer his
mother might have become more open. He silently set the table
for dinner as she had asked. When he finished he walked to the
kitchen door.

"I won't be having dinner tonight, Mam. I'm going over to
Finnuala to see how she is and we're heading down to the disco
later. I haven't seen the gang since I came home."

Immediately Alice's face brightened. "Now there's a grand
girl. Finnuala, yes you go talk to her Michael, she's a nice girl. I
heard she got a place in the civil service too, a good pensionable
job. Don't be saying things like that to her, don't be putting her
off. Her mother and father are grand respectable people."

Michael stared at his mother, realising that she had not grasped
one bit of what he had told her. Small-town Catholic Ireland had
done a great job on her; she was able to sweep under the carpet
anything that did not conform to the norm. If he ever needed
proof that he could no longer live in his childhood home, he had
it now. He went upstairs to get ready for the disco.

END OF AUGUST, 1986

"IT'S NOT Pearse O'Connor, that hairy brute on legs, is it?"
Padraig exclaimed, raising his eyebrows.

"Sssh, keep your voice down" Cormac whispered. "You're
right. It's not him, because it's over."

"What's wrong? Is he not able to keep up with a young fellow like you? Ten years of a difference, Cormac, it's a lot on a man's body."

"Enough, Padraig, it's over. In actual fact he's getting married." Quickly scanning the small coffee shop to make sure no one else was listening, he continued. "A shotgun job. His girlfriend is pregnant and he's doing the right thing and standing by her."

"Oh, my God, Pearse O'Connor, I can't believe it," Padraig said. "His mother gets her hair done with us. She's a real witch if ever I saw one."

Their meeting in Callan's' coffee shop had been planned to discuss the trip to London. While Padraig was buzzing with excitement at the adventure ahead, Cormac was having second thoughts.

"He's a mad gambler, Cormac. You're well off without him. He never has a shilling. Only for his woman having that good pensionable job in the library they'd have nothing. You're well off without him."

"But it was great, I thought he loved me. We had such a connection. It was amazing sex, just mind-blowing,"

"Will you get real?" Padraig said, placing his cup down firmly on the table. "Harden up, relationships come and go. It's all about the action. Get it while you can, that's my motto in life. Just think about all the action ahead of us in London."

Padraig could see that he was failing to lift his friend's spirits. "When is the wedding, anyway?" he asked.

"It's next week."

"So that means all the ladies will be getting their hair done in our salon, doesn't it?" Padraig's mind was racing ahead, and a plan was starting to form.

"I'd say so, Padraig. I don't really care."

"Look that's the way it is, Cormac. You just have to get on with it. Tomorrow night we'll have a ball, our last night as a big gang at the Subterranean and then back to Alan's house, so c'mon, think ahead. You have to be strong."

Just before they left, he looked straight at Cormac. "Leave Pearse O'Connor's wedding to me. I have something in mind that'll make her never forget her son's wedding."

THE WOMEN came and went in their droves for their colour, wash, blow-drys and cuts on the busy Friday. Padraig knew he wouldn't miss the place, apart from some of the older regulars whom he liked, but the thought of leaving his sister Martha pained him and he felt his nerve beginning to wane. Once Mrs O'Connor, Pearse's mother, arrived at the salon, however, he put all these thoughts aside; he knew what he had to do.

The salon was a small room made up of two wash basins, three leather chairs facing their own mirrors and a work station, and on the other side of the room was a bench where the women waited in line. Leading off this room was a small toilet, together with a shelving area containing the salon's stock of colours, peroxides, shampoos and conditioners. Although the women pretended to be immersed in their glossy magazines, everyone could hear everyone else in the salon. While he was blow-drying a customer's hair, Padraig could hear "Haghead Dinah", his boss, gossiping with Mrs O'Connor. There was no mention, of course, of "shotgun" or "rush job" with regard to the forthcoming wedding. The story for all the customers to hear was that the sudden marriage between Pearse and Jackie was for tax purposes, and a major rebate was in order if they tied the knot before the end of September.

As he had expected, once he was finished with his customer, Dinah ordered him to organise Mrs O'Connor's colour. "It will be my pleasure," he said, causing Dinah to give him a strange look, wondering if he was being sarcastic.

As he applied every last drop of the mixture to Mrs O'Connor's head, embedding the colour deep into the hairline, Padraig robotically chatted to her. Placing cotton wool right around her hairline so the colour wouldn't drip onto her face, he then covered her head with a tight plastic bag to ensure the colour would take.

"It'll take twenty minutes," he said as he placed her under the dryer. He didn't hang around for her impatient comments about all she had to do for the wedding but lit a cigarette and headed for the storeroom area. After checking that the coast was clear, he gathered the large plastic containers, each holding hair colours identified by large numbering on their labels. He proceeded to mix the colours; sixes becoming twos, sevens becoming number ones. He poured the peroxide down the sink and replaced it with conditioner, which would ensure that when Dinah wanted to colour the customer's hair with peroxide, none of the colours would take properly. With his nerves jangling in his stomach, yet driven on by a rush of adrenalin, he walked back into the salon, checked his watch and knew it was now or never.

"We're out of milk Dinah. I'll pop across the road and get some for the tea. I'll just get my coat." Since it was a busy Friday morning, the till was bulging with notes. Pretending to take a few coins for the milk, he lifted the exact amount of his wages and slyly wrapped the notes tightly in his hand. "I'll take Mrs O'Connor's colour off first," he said. Dinah nodded and continued talking to her own customer. Slipping his favourite scissors, comb and his wages into his pocket, Padraig proceeded to wash off the colour from Mrs O'Connor's head and, having immediately placed a towel over her, calmly moved her to his work station. He slowly peeled the towel from her head and threw it on the floor. The whole salon gasped. Mrs O'Connor became aware everyone was staring at her with their mouths open and put on her glasses..

"Aaagh" was the only thing that came out of her mouth as she looked with horror in the mirror at the sight of her hair like that of a witch on Halloween night, the dark purple colour in stark contrast to her white, pasty face. As she continued to scream, Padraig leaned towards her right ear and whispered, "It's a witch's colour for a witch,"

Dinah regained her composure and ran towards Mrs O'Connor. In the confusion Padraig stepped back, collected his coat from the coat-stand and ran out the front door of the salon. He laughed out loud to himself as he broke into a run, heading towards the park down by the river where he was to meet Siobhan. They planned to have a few drinks from the off-licence before they headed to the disco later with the whole gang. He smiled to himself, thinking of the small note he had written that morning and left in the till for Dinah.

Dear D "Old Slapper", Got my wages, which were owed to me. Hope you have a colourful wedding. Hated working here. Bye forever. P.

"GO HANDY on that stuff, Siobhan. We've a long night ahead." Padraig watched Siobhan neck down a naggin of vodka. They were both sitting in the park with drink from the off-licence before heading off to the Subterranean, having left their bags for London in the shed in the back garden of Alan's house.

Padraig was afraid she would get aggressive if she got too drunk. "Did you hear Finnuala passed her medical?" he asked casually. "She's starting in the civil service as a clerical assistant."

"Oh, that's riveting," Siobhan said, taking another slug of vodka, then adding, "I'm sorry, I take that back, Finnuala is lovely. It'll be good for her. C'mon let's get some chips and sober me up."

The disco was in full action when they arrived at nine o'clock.

Just inside, a bouncer stood in front of Siobhan. "No messing from you tonight, none of your fighting." Padraig was quick to dart a look at Siobhan to warn her keep her mouth shut. Fat Mark was playing The Clash, which went down well with all the gang who had gathered together at a large table in the corner which was already teeming with drinks.

"The house is ready," Alan announced. "Me mum and dad have been farmed out, well they're staying in me brother's tonight, so everyone bring their own drink and make sure we get a few extra flagons of cider on the way home."

Mary Rose and her new Garda boyfriend Tom had joined the group by getting two small stools and sitting at the edge of the table. She snuggled as closely as she could to his bulky frame.

"He seems all right," Michael whispered to Siobhan, "especially for a cop."

"I hate cops," Siobhan announced drunkenly, loud enough so that Tom heard.

"Oh, you hate cops, do you?" Tom replied loudly. "You'd be happy enough if something went wrong, you'd need us cops then." Siobhan stood to square up to him. Within seconds he stood up also and together they faced each other over the table.

"Now, now come on let's enjoy ourselves, relax." Michael said, but before he could take control of the situation Big Head Jock, the main bouncer, came over shouting, "That's enough now, I'll have none of this. Siobhan, you're always starting trouble. Any hassle and you're out."

"What do you mean it's my fault?" she screamed. "He started it!" Knowing that it would impress Mary Rose, Tom immediately flashed his Garda card, which had gained him free entry to the disco.

"Any trouble here tonight. I'll get the lads in," Tom said. "Us cops know how to deal with Fatima Whitbread lookalikes." Tom

78

guffawed and gave a sideways glance to Mary Rose, hoping she would appreciate his joke. For Siobhan it was one insult too far. Glasses smashed everywhere as she lunged across the drink-laden table at Tom. Big Head Jock stepped quickly between the two of them but then let out a groan of pain as Siobhan's right hand made contact with him.

"You stupid cow, what have you done?" Michael shouted, staring at the scene. "C'mon get out of here." There was a scatter as Michael caught Siobhan by the shoulder and ran towards the door. The others grabbed their belongings and followed. Fat Mark began to shout from the stage through his microphone, "Siobhan, you're barred for life, never darken this door again."

They scuttled down the main street towards the off-licence on the way to Alan's house. When they were a safe distance from the disco they stopped and all roared with laughter.

"You're some woman" was all Alan could say. "I left a full pint there on that table. Thank God you didn't hit the guard or you'd be in the police cell for the night."

"I think you broke his nose you know, he's out cold," Cormac said in shock. "I never thought a woman could do that to a man."

"He asked for it," Siobhan giggled. "Been threatening to do that for years."

Back at the disco, Mary Rose was left to pick up the pieces as she consoled Tom, patting him on the shoulder. "Don't mind her, she's a psycho anyway. She's away to London in the morning with the rest of the gang. We're well rid of her." Tom knew he had a lucky escape, looking at the state of Big Head Jock, blood streaming from his nose.

In Alan's house the music played loudly as they all got stuck into the endless cans of beer and spirits from the off-licence, along with some extra strong hash Alan had got hold of. Siobhan was now the hero of the night as they joked and laughed about seeing

Big Head Jock out cold on the floor. After a couple of hours of revelling a mellow atmosphere fell over the house. Alan had an attack of the munchies and headed for the kitchen. Cormac was now quite sozzled and fell asleep on the sofa. Siobhan and Padraig were busy whispering to each other in the corner.

Finnuala led a drunken Michael upstairs to Alan's bedroom.

"POOR MRS O'Connor," Siobhan tittered, "she's probably scarred for life with the mixture of colours you put on her scalp. I'm sure it's burned and in bits at this stage"

"Oh yeah, sure," Padraig said, smiling back at her, "it'll be weeping at this stage. I'd say the head is burned off her. They'll be in the salon this morning trying to get the colour changed, if her hair hasn't fallen out by now."

"I suppose she could wear a wig for the wedding," Siobhan said as if offering a solution to a problem.

It was eight o'clock on Saturday morning and the ferry had been out on the Irish Sea for the past hour; the swell of the sea was gathering strength as the ship ploughed its way against a strong headwind. Still groggy from the drink, drugs and lack of sleep, the five friends had managed to drag themselves from Alan's to get a bus at six o'clock to Dun Laoghaire for the crossing to Holyhead. The final leg to London would be a bus trip of several hours, the cheapest option available to them, but as the ferry was only half full they had managed to secure the comfortable seats at no extra cost.

"At least it will give them something else to talk about besides 'the death has occurred,' Padraig said, referring to the local death notices announced every morning at nine o'clock on the radio, which all the customers eagerly tuned into every day. He was trying to hide his sadness at leaving his sister behind. He hadn't

80

told his father anything, but knew that his sister would tell him the news that morning.

"No doubt Dinah will call to my house later on," he added, "trying to find out where I am and looking for some compensation from him."

"Your father could always pay her in kind," Siobhan giggled.

"I wonder when your dad will get your letter," Padraig said, bringing Siobhan back to reality with a jolt.

"Well, I did tell him I was staying overnight at a friend's, so I suppose later today when he realises I'm not home he'll look around and see the letter I've written for him. It's short and sweet, Padraig, to the point."

"Go on, tell me again, what did you say to him?"

"It was something to the effect, 'Gone to London for a few months, don't worry. The widow, Mrs O'Brien, across the road will take care of you. Need my space Dad, you can't do anything, I'm over eighteen. Love Siobhan.' "

"I didn't know he had a thing with Mrs O'Brien, the widow woman."

"I can see his face right now, I can hear him announcing the words 'space, big world, such notions, these young people, they get too much.' " Siobhan was delighted that she had stood up to her dad, even if it wasn't directly.

"Your man is off again." Padraig nodded towards Cormac who was sitting in the next seat. They both looked at Cormac whose face had the look of a child lost in the supermarket as he sat alone crying softly,.

"He'll be fine," Siobhan whispered. "Cormac always likes a good cry, especially when too much drink has been taken."

"My head is starting to open," Padraig announced. "I think the drink is wearing off." He looked at Siobhan. "Let' go and see if we can find a bar open. I'm sure we can buy a pint or two now that we are out at sea. C'mon." They headed towards the bar area, leaving the others there sitting sombrely, each lost in their own thoughts.

MARY ROSE looked around her small box-bedroom full of pink frills and fluffy pillows. It was early in the morning, just getting bright as she snuggled down under the covers to keep herself warm. Closing her eyes again she allowed her mind to wander back to the night before. Thank God that jumped-up Michael Duffy and all that gang were gone. That was an infantile party they had planned last night, and to imagine that they thought she would go! She had much more important things to do and bigger fish to fry, namely her new boyfriend Tom. She knew from going out with him over the past five weeks that he was smitten with her. He was a country boy from the West of Ireland and his ramblings about hurling and GAA football held no interest for her, but she had long perfected the art of looking interested even though her mind was on other things. Things like Tom's long-term ambitions in the police force and his promotional prospects. She had skilfully wheedled the information from him and was glad to discover that he was interested in joining the Special Branch in Dublin.

Their date had gone well until they joined Michael and the gang. That Siobhan really was a lunatic. Outrageously, after the others had been kicked out of the disco, the bouncers had tried to make herself and Tom leave, until he flashed his Garda badge again, and immediately they took a totally different attitude towards them. They stayed a while more in the club drinking and then went back to her parents' house. She had decided she would allow him to go the full way with her on the sofa. Afterwards, with her virginal state shattered, she wondered what all the fuss was about. It had been rough, very fast, with Tom doing a lot of loud thrusting, groaning and grunting. The whole business only took a few minutes, after which Tom fell asleep almost immediately and she had trouble getting him off her. When Mary Rose did manage to peel herself from underneath she stood and looked down at him. His snoring was so loud she was afraid her mother and father would come down, so she held his nose to wake him. Contentedly he left to return to the rented house that he shared with other young guards.

As she lay snuggled under the blanket, Mary Rose began to pick out engagement rings in her mind. She wondered if guards got allowances for engagement rings and weddings and such expenses. She knew they got expenses for almost everything else. She must check Tom's contract and have a good read of the small print. Her job in Dublin in the bank would do her for the moment but she would eventually be a Mrs Superintendent or even a Mrs Chief Inspector. She felt she was now on the right track to making this happen. Turning over in her warm bed she knew she had taken the first steps, especially if her period didn't come. Tom would then be forced to do the right thing and marry her. A woman had to use all her resources to get what she wanted in this life. A price had to be paid for everything.

CORMAC SAT in the big leather Pulman seat on the ferry, his hold-all at his feet. He had hardly stopped crying since they left: no major sobs or wails, just slow-flowing tears which he was always able to conjure up at will when his emotions demanded it. He thought about how his mother had cried when he had left the house on Friday night. He would miss her but no one else, apart from Pearse, of course. The tears welled up in his eyes even more as he thought about Pearse getting married in a few days' time.

He wasn't quite sure why he was on the boat to London. He

just knew he wanted to go somewhere, anywhere to escape from Dunglass. His mother had given him a tenner and promised she would post him the weekly newspaper once he got an address. He knew she would put a tenner in the newspaper every week, and was happy at the thought. He wondered if he would make it home by Christmas, as he had promised, but then he thought of how Pearse's girlfriend would be well into her pregnancy by then and how a baby would follow soon after, an event that would no doubt put his lover beyond his reach forever. The thought stabbed him deeply, and with a soft whimper he returned to nurture his tears, convinced no one understood his pain.

Alan sat in the next seat, still feeling mellow from the joint he had smoked just before they had got on the bus to Dublin. He wasn't sure what to expect of London, but he felt glad of the chance to get away as he wanted to teach his parents a lesson. They needed to miss him for a while as they were taking him for granted. As the youngest and the only one left at home, he believed he was entitled to the family home and his parents' money as soon as they died, which he felt couldn't be much longer considering they were in their seventies. His father had handed him his full pension money as soon as he had picked it up from the local Post Office.

"There you are, Alan, take this money and always know that you can come home anytime," he said. "This is always your home."

"Oh thanks, Dad, you're so kind," Alan said as his lower lip trembled with perfect timing. He thought of suggesting to his dad that a trip to the solicitors together could be arranged when he was be home at Christmas but he decided to leave that for another time. His one immediate regret was that he couldn't bring any of his stash of hash with him on the boat, as he didn't want to take his chances with the English police. As soon as they were in London he would speak to the first black person he met in the street. He could ask them where their local drug supplier lived; after all, everyone knew that all black people were Rastafarian, so they must smoke the stuff. Alan smiled to himself, thinking of the mega new apartment waiting for him in London, the extra special hash that must be there, and the freedom to do exactly as he wished. He fell asleep happily thinking of all the wonderful things that were in store for him.

FINNUALA LAY in her bed thinking of Michael. It was nine in the morning, so he would be halfway over the Irish Sea by now. He had told her the previous night how things had changed since he had gone to New York where he had met a man and now he was sure he was gay. But Finnuala wasn't convinced. And what had happened at the party had given her a glimmer of hope that she could change him. After leading Michael like a child to the bedroom in Alan's house, all she wanted to do at first was to just hold him, to feel him close to her. But a clinch had turned into a full embrace, then arousal and after a few moments of fumbling and touching each other they had full intercourse.

A few hours later, Michael had got up and gone downstairs without saying a word. Finnuala followed down later and embraced each of her friends as they were about to leave, reserving a special lingering hug for Michael, hoping that he would say something about what had happened, but all he gave was a fond goodbye. After they had all left she went home to get a few hours' rest. But she couldn't sleep, feeling bereft after her friends' departure and especially that of the man she loved so dearly. Tomorrow she would do something she had never done before: she would start a special novena for Michael to return home to her – and for her period to come.

MICHAEL FELT light-headed as he sat in silence on the ferry. The swell of the sea had become stronger, and his stomach was moving up and down with the dipping and rolling of the ship. He tried not to think about his stomach as he watched other passengers swaying from one side of the corridor to the other. The smell of vomit hit his nostrils as he saw someone getting sick on the floor.

Michael's emotions were as unsettled as his stomach. He felt excited at the thought of a new life in London, but sadness at the memory of his mother crying as he left the house, and a deep resentment towards his father who had left for work early in order to avoid saying goodbye properly, which had hurt him deeply. He thought of Finnuala and their embrace in Alan's bedroom. He had been very drunk and stoned, and had just followed her, delighted to lie down on the bed for a while. Surprisingly one thing had led to another and there had been a connection. Michael felt regret at leaving Finnuala; he did love her but not in the way she wanted. He would write to her very soon and explaining his feelings.

The excitement he felt about London and the course in shoe design was, he had to admit to himself, tinged with apprehension. But there was one certainty: no matter what happened, there was no going back.

LONDON

THE FIVE of them emerged bedraggled and hungover from the bus at Victoria Station in the West End of London. After wandering around aimlessly through the nearby streets for a while they found a cafe where they revived themselves with cups of coffee and did their best to get their bearings with the aid of an Underground map Michael had grabbed at the bus station. They then split up. The plan was that Alan and Cormac would head to Kilburn to stay with Alan's aunt until Michael was able to arrange accommodation for everyone in Hackney, following a lead that Pearl had told him about in a letter.

Michael was keeping his fingers crossed that everything would work out with the accommodation. Pearl had explained in her letter that she had been in touch with her friend Karen, who had a "squat" in Hackney, and that she was expecting them and would help them find something. Michael wasn't sure what a "squat" meant and didn't know what to expect, but he knew Pearl wouldn't let him down.

The two boys split for Kilburn, while he, Siobhan and Padraig took a tube to Hackney and made their final journey on foot, dragging their luggage behind them until they finally located Charles Park, a small complex of drab brown-bricked council flats, each building five storeys high.

"This is a fair kip of a place," Padraig whispered as they passed a gang of teenagers gathered on the corner who eye-balled them darkly from underneath their hoods.

They found the building called Charlestown House and climbed the stairs to the second floor. The interior, with its dark corridor and dank smell, was as unwelcoming as the outside. Nervously, Michael knocked on the door of Number 6.

The friendly smiling face of a pretty young woman with brown curly hair opened the door to them. "You must be Michael. Hi, I'm Karen," she said as she ushered them into the flat, which Michael could immediately see was pleasantly furnished and well kept.

They sat around for a while, chatting excitedly. Karen explained that she had been in London for two years, working as a waitress, and lived with her boyfriend Tom, who was from Dublin and worked on the building sites. Michael told her all the news he had about Pearl, how they had met in New York, and how he hoped she would be coming to London. As they talked, he wondered when he could raise the matter of finding accommodation, but though it might be bad mannered to ask immediately. He was glad then when Karen brought it up herself.

"Listen, I know you're all probably anxious about getting somewhere to stay," she said. "You'll be able to find a place okay, but until you do, you are welcome to stay here." They thanked her profusely, and Michael felt a sense of relief sweep over him.

Answering Michael's questions, she proceeded to explain what "squatting" was all about. It was a common practice in London, she said, and meant that you could take over an abandoned council flat as long as it couldn't be proved that you had made a forcible entry, and the council would generally turn a blind to you staying there unless you became a troublemaker. She and Tom had been squatting in their flat for over a year now.

"In fact, there's a flat vacant right now on the ground floor," she said, " but it's in really awful shape as the last people to have it were a crowd of heroin junkies, and there's one also, just as bad, on the fourth floor. You'll definitely have to get both of them fumigated as, God knows, there'll be plenty of fleas, and maybe even worse. Maybe you can get something better if you look around, so don't rush into anything. As I say, feel welcome to stay with us for a few days until you get organised."

They continued to sit around drinking tea and chatting until Karen's boyfriend Tom returned home. He was friendly but didn't say much except to give them the low-down again on squatting as well as advice about signing on for the dole. Karen made a meal, not long after which the three friends fell asleep, their excitement finally overcome by tiredness, Siobhan using the one spare bedroom and Michael and Padraig stretched out on two sofas.

88

AS KAREN had suggested, they took a few days to explore the area, mainly trying to find out about other vacant flats, but after failing to find something suitable they decided they would go for the ground floor flat she had mentioned and tell Alan and Cormac about the one on the fourth floor. Tom helped them to break into the flat with a crowbar and then change the locks to disguise any signs of forced entry. He also gave them the number of a company that did fumigating, which Michael rang.

"How much does fumigating it cost again?" Siobhan asked as the three of them stood looking around at the filth in the empty squat.

"I told you already, Siobhan," Michael said. "It's eighty pounds, but they'll do a full fumigation of the whole place. It will be worth it." He was trying to sound as confident as he could.

"Well. I've an interview for that job, so I'll be heading," Padraig announced, not wishing to stay any longer in the stench of the flat.

There was a knock on the front door. The three of looked at each other like children caught doing something bold.

"You're lucky to get us, mate, we were in the area for the council," a burly man said when Michael opened the door. He was dressed in full protective gear and with a gas mask hanging around his neck. He walked past Michael towards the kitchen area followed by another man similarly attired. "Best to get out, mate, while we fumigate the place, and come back in a few hours." Michael, Padraig and Siobhan scuttled out to the landing outside the flat. One of the men called after them, "It will be a full day before the poisons work, so best you don't stay here for at least two nights."

The three of them stood staring at each other for a moment on the cold communal landing. A wave of apprehension hit Michael, but he thought of Dunglass and his father's face and with that he put a confident smile on his face.

"C'mon Siobhan," he said, "let's go back to Karen's flat, get our papers and go down to the dole office. Padraig, we can meet you later, after your interview. I told Alan and Cormac we'd meet them at the post office on Caledonian Road later before heading to The Nag's Head and fill them in on the squat on the fourth floor. They can organise the fumigation guys. It should all be settled by the end of the week."

Siobhan nodded, ready to follow orders from Michael.

"Look lads, I'm starting college in a couple of days so we have to get things organised, so its all systems go. Karen said there's a shop down near the pub where we can buy foam sheets, big thick ones. They are cut by the yard and we can use them as mattresses, so we can get them on the way home."

Padraig looked at Michael trying to think of something funny to say. The flat was like a bomb hit it, but Michael was right; after a few days and a bit of organising things would improve. "You'd know your dad was in the army, a sergeant major," he said. Michael looked quizzically at him. Padraig threw in his punch-line with a smile as he headed off. "What's in the cat is in the kitten."

SIOBHAN'S STOMACH was in a knot as they entered the dole office, a dismal, scruffy place with lino floors, no heaters and the paint peeling from the walls. Her heart sank when she saw four long queues leading up to the hatches where the staff were seated behind thick, reinforced glass.

"It's a long way from Woolworth's, Michael," she said as they joined a queue.

"We're here for the long haul, Siobhan. Signing on is just part of the deal. C'mon, let's not think too much about home at this stage." Michael looked at her reassuringly. "Have you got your birth certificate?" he asked, trying to distract her.

90

"Yeah, I have. I have everything here." They stood in silence for a long time, watching the four queues move at snail's pace. As they approached the top, a young woman at the next hatch started to scream at the top of her voice.

"I need to feed my fucking baby, I've got no money, where's my Giro?" The small baby in her arms started to cry loudly, and a toddler clung to her legs. Siobhan could see the fat woman behind the counter throwing her eyes to heaven.

"Heard it all before, love. Go to information hatch number six." The distraught young woman gathered up her toddler in her other arm and made her way to another long line at a different hatch. Siobhan heard "Next", and it was her turn.

"Address?" the civil servant asked in a strong English accent.

"Number 4, Charlestown House, Charles Park Estate, Hackney, and here's my birth certificate." Siobhan handed over her documents. The woman took a fleeting look at them, another at Siobhan and filled in some forms. She rose from her desk, walked over to the filing cabinet behind the counter, and Siobhan's heart was in her mouth for a few moments. When the woman came back she robotically slid a sheet through the hatch for Siobhan to sign.

"Make sure you register in the Job Centre," she said. Siobhan had hardly signed the sheet when the woman barked out, "Next!"

"When will I get my money?" Siobhan dared to ask.

"Should be in two weeks. It will be sent by post, the Giro. Now next!"

Siobhan headed outside to wait for Michael. She breathed in the city air deeply, a welcome replacement for the dense, stale air of the dole office. Dunglass now felt like another planet as she watched the speeding traffic go by in both directions on Caledonian Road. Within ten minutes Michael joined her and said they should go to the Job Centre straight away and get everything thing sorted out, sooner rather than later.

The Job Centre was upbeat, full of smiling assistants encouraging Michael and Siobhan to have a look at the job descriptions listed there, one of which was for an assistant at a gym, which made Siobhan's eyes light up instantly. They helped them to fill out forms and encouraged them to go for interviews in the next couple of days. Michael played the game, smiling and nodding at the appropriate time, but had no intentions of getting a job at this stage with college starting in a few days. Outside, he lit up a cigarette, then exhaled the smoke with a deep sense of satisfaction.. "At least we're in the system now," he said, happy that there was another thing done and off his list.

"I wonder how Padraig got on," Siobhan said as they walked towards The Nag's Head. "Do you think he got the job?"

AS HE opened the door of the "Cut and Style" salon a bell tinkled to signal his entrance. He had seen the ad in the window looking for a stylist the day before when he, Michael and Siobhan had gone for a walk to escape the confined space of Karen's flat. It was on a small street just off Caledonian Road, which was only twenty minutes walk from the squat, so it would be amazing to get the job. As he stood inside the door, his stomach was in a knot and he tried to appear more confident than he felt.

"Can I help you, dear?" A plump woman in her mid-fifties who looked the double of Bet Lynch in "Coronation Street" came towards him, her large boobs bouncing up and down.

"I'm Denise, can I help you?"

"I'm here for the job interview." Padraig stumbled on his words. "I mean, I saw the ad in the window, you're looking for a stylist." She puffed heavily on her cigarette as she smiled.

"Come this way, darling." She brought Padraig through the

small salon where he noticed there were three stylists' chairs and one sink to the right where a young girl was busy washing the hair of a customer.

"That's Nuala, our assistant" Denise said. "What's your name, darling?"

"I'm Padraig," he said as he extended his hand.

She led him out to the back room where she asked him a few simple questions about where he had trained. He was worried that she would ask for a reference, which would be difficult after what had happened on his last day at work in Dunglass, but after putting on the kettle and making tea she began to talk about herself, spilling out her whole life story in ten minutes. Divorced three times, she had a love for dark-skinned men, especially Egyptian – "Something about their eyes, darling."

Padraig looked at her in awe. He knew he would like this woman: a kind heart, but hard as nails.

"Men are like buses, darling, there's always another one around the corner in ten minutes. What about you, darling, where are you living? You're Irish obviously with an accent like that."

"I'm not long off the boat, wanted to escape the small town I've come from, and a few of us are living in a flat up in Charles Park Estate." He didn't want to say that fumigation men were currently clearing it out.

"I can cut, colour and style, Denise. I'm ready to work and could start in the morning and would love if you would give me a trial run." Padraig ran off the interview speech he had prepared the previous night.

"Well, it's mostly regulars here, and Nuala our assistant is doing her training, so let's give it a shot and you can start at nine o'clock in the morning."

Padraig was on a high as he left the salon, thrilled to have secured a job so quickly. "One in your eye Dad, one in your eye," he said to himself as he skipped up the street towards the pub to meet the others.

Michael and Siobhan met Alan and Cormac at the post office on Caledonian Road before heading to The Nag's Head. Alan began to whinge and complain from the moment they met.

"It's not exactly what I thought it would be, Michael. I can't get over the size of the place, its huge, London. It's like a never-ending concrete jungle, non-stop buildings." Michael ignored him as they headed to the pub.

It was early afternoon and the pub, which reeked of stale cigarette smoke, had a few older hardened drinkers at the bar. They bought drinks and sat down away from everyone at the far end, in the small snug area.

"It's a bit steep, eighty pounds," Alan said after Michael told them the cost for fumigation if they wanted to move into the flat on the fourth floor.

"Well, it is full fumigation, Alan, and it's up to you. You can stay at your aunt's for the rest of your life if you want. All I know is there is a squat up there free. You can get it organised tomorrow and you can move in two days. We've been down to the dole office and the Job Centre, so the sooner you have an address the sooner you two can do the same and get out of your aunt's way."

"Okay, okay," Alan said, knowing that he had annoyed Michael.

"Wonder how the wedding went," Cormac piped in. The others stared, and for a moment didn't realise what he was talking about. Cormac's mind was still back in Dunglass. No one answered him.

"I hear it's a bit of a war zone, that estate," Alan said. "Do you think we could get somewhere else?"

"Look, Alan, I don't care what you do.," Michael said. "You've made the decision to come here to London. You've got to make the best of it. None of us have money for deposits for flats in nice places where your aunt lives in Kilburn or Islington. All I know is we're making the best of it. Now you can stay or you can go home. Enough complaining."

"Don't be so dramatic," Cormac said. "C'mon it's just a bit different from Ireland."

"No one makes eye contact," Alan said. "It's a bit strange, that's all I'm saying."

"Well it's either toughen up or go home," Michael said. "The choice is yours. All I know is that I ain't going back."

Just then Padraig made his entrance with a flourish and floated across the pub to join the gang.

"Got the job, start in the morning," he said with a big grin on his face. "Why don't we go on the lash, go up the West End, get us some action."

"You've to start work in the morning, Padraig," Siobhan said, "and you don't want to start your first day with the eyes hanging out of your head. We have to go and get those mattresses, so no, we'll have to leave the West End until the weekend after we get in to our flats."

"Wonder where we could get some hash," Alan whispered into the centre of the circle of friends. "The first black person I see at the estate I'll ask them. They always know where to get it. They all smoke it."

"What makes you think that?" Michael asked in an irritated voice.

"Well, they're all into Bob Marley, so being Rastafarian they must smoke it."

Michael shook his head, dismissing Alan, and suggested that they all finish their drinks. "It's time to head back to the flat and see how the guys are getting on with the fumigation. Have you got your money, Alan? You can pay them now."

With that, Michael gave them all the nod, and they followed him, the leader, back to the squat.

"I HOPE this is worth the trek, Padraig. I've got to go to work and I don't have that long." Michael was anxious as they sat together on the tube. He had found a job in a gay bar called First Out, right in the heart of Tottenham Court Road, where he was being paid under the counter so he could still get his fortnightly Giro.

"Don't be getting waspy with me, Michael," Padraig said. "I'm told that the shoes are pretty amazing there, so it'll be good for research purposes." He had been a few times to the Cock and Hen Club where a lot of the men dressed in women's clothes. Most of them, he discovered, had bought their outfits and shoes in a shop near Oxford Circus. "Don't you just love London?" he had said excitedly when first telling Michael about the shop and persuading him to visit it with him.

Over the past few weekends he and the others had been out to experience the freedom on offer in the gay club scene. Sex was readily available, and Padraig rarely turned down the opportunity of a quick encounter. Eye contact was all that was necessary, a nod and wink and straight into the toilets or down to the darkened room at the back.

Up from the underground, they walked a couple of streets until they came across the shop which had "Fantasy Style" written in ornate writing overhead. Two mannequins displayed pink and black dresses in the window, the front of which was lined with large-sized shoes and boots along with a sign saying "Sizes 8 to 16 available". Inside, the shop was crammed with extra-large evening wear on one side, larger coats on the opposite, and right in the middle were rails full of glitzy evening wear, tops and blouses. Just to the left of the front door was a tall stand displaying rows of platform shoes, boots and high heels. Michael made a beeline to the shoes and picked them up lovingly one by one.

"Oh my God," he said out loud. "Look at the design of these, Padraig."

"They're amazing aren't they," the man behind the counter said with a smile. "We do all sizes and can order them in from China and Italy." He extended his hand to Michael, having instantly recognised a fellow lover of shoes. He introduced himself as Declan; he was the owner of the shop and was from Kilkenny but had lived in London for ten years. As Michael and he became immersed in a conversation about the sizes and patterns available, Padraig explored the shop and its dresses, his mind already racing ahead as he visualised his alter ego, Shiel O'Blige, in each of the evening dresses. Touching the texture of the velvet, the sequins, the frills, he was gobsmacked.

"They're pretty amazing, aren't they?" Declan could read Padraig's mind. "Every time I come in I get the same feeling. Would you like to try on one of the frocks?"

Almost afraid to leave his fantasy zone, Padraig reluctantly answered, "I haven't got time today, but another day I will. I heard about your shop down in the Cock and Hen Club, they all talk about it."

"Most of our customers are regulars there. They come in for all their clothes. We can order in anything special that is required, and we can also accept instalments so you can pay off on the stuff." Declan moved around the shop as he spoke, automatically tidying up some of the blouses and dresses.

A question suddenly sprung into Padraig's mind out of nowhere. "Do you ever get customers looking for tips on make-up and style and what would suit them?"

Declan stopped what he was doing and looked intently at Padraig, sizing him up and down. "Now, that's interesting," he said.

"The fact is that I do get quite a number looking for advice, but I don't have the time or the skill to provide it. Do you have something in mind?"

Padraig was doing his best not to let his excitement bubble over.

"I'm a make up artist and a hairdresser, not long in London. I did my make-up course in Dublin, where I also did a lot of work with men. I can bring in my certificate from my course if you want."

Declan went silent for a few moments, looking at Padraig and thinking. Eventually, he said, "There's a room out the back, I'm sure we could arrange something if you wanted to set up and do a class. We could take it from there, see how it goes. You can put a poster in the window."

Padraig's mind was buzzing, and he wanted to stay longer and chat about the idea but saw Michael pointing to his watch and knew that they had less than a half hour before his shift started in the bar. Declan handed Padraig his card and told him to come back with something for the window as soon as he could..

"Wasn't the footwear amazing, such detail on the heels?" Michael continued to rave about the footwear as they made their way back to the tube station, but Padraig hardly listened, his mind taken up with organising his new make-up classes for men and wondering how he would shape the poster. He headed to the bar with Michael to have a beer before he headed back to the squat. They chatted for a while as Michael started work. "Style by P" was the title they both agreed on as they planned Padraig's poster for the window of the shop.

MICHAEL HAD become a hoarder, gathering lots of bits and pieces for the flat. The latest addition was a chaise longue which had been spotted in a skip and which he, Padraig and Siobhan had rolled back noisily on its castor wheels at two in the morning. He and Siobhan now lounged on it in front of the gas fire in Michael's room. It was Saturday night and they were planning to head up to the West End. Michael made no complaints when Alan and Cormac joined them, sitting on the floor in front of the chaise longue.

"All work and no play," Alan said as he took another swig from a flagon of cider.

"I don't know if I'll go down the West End," Siobhan said, looking at Cormac. She and Cormac liked going to the movies a lot or staying in, as they were not that fond of the club scene and all the madness that went with it..

"I've to get up early in the morning and open the gym," she said. "Sunday morning is a rush hour for all those fitness fanatics." They all burst out laughing as they passed around another joint.

"Ah, c'mon, come with us, please," Michael said. "We'll all go up together and you can get the late bus home with Cormac if you don't want to stay too long." Siobhan had been in the West End a few times, but most of the gay bars were for men and as yet she hadn't found a bar where she could feel at ease with other women.

"Wear your Doc Martins and bring your truncheon," Michael said. Walking through Hangman's Alley, the short cut from the bus, at one o'clock in the morning would be dangerous, even for a big woman like Siobhan. At Michael's instruction they had all invested in hobnail boots for self-protection, and Siobhan carried a small truncheon at all times in a small hold-all on her shoulder.

"C'mon, Padraig, get a move on," Michael shouted into Padraig who was busy in his bedroom getting ready. "We're going soon, so hurry up. All the cider will be gone."

"Be there in a mo," Padraig called back in a muffled voice.

"That Harry Head sure has good stuff," Alan said, inhaling deeply on the joint. He was referring to his local supplier. "Wonder has he other gear?" He passed the joint onto Siobhan who refused and said she would stick to the cider.

The door opened and Padraig made his entrance, causing them all to open their mouths in shock. They had been used to seeing Shiel O'Blige around the flat on an odd evening, but he hadn't yet had the courage to go out in public like this. He was wearing a short black shiny dress, his bony knees protruding through silky tights above high-heeled black patent shoes, the whole ensemble finished off with over-the-elbow black gloves that contrasted strongly with a short white fur jacket. A blond shoulder-length wig together with impeccably applied make-up and ruby-red glossy lips gave the desired dramatic effect. He stood posing, his hairless chest enhanced by the two pairs of rugby socks he had stuffed under his bra.

"Hi guys," Padraig said with a big smile on his face.

"Wow," was all Michael could manage to say. Cormac was speechless and Siobhan burst into a fit of laughter.

"You're not going out looking like that," Alan piped in "What if you get your head kicked in? There's queer bashers all over London."

Padraig was defiant. "This is London, mate. Look at me funny and I'll scratch your eyes out." It seemed strange for a beautiful looking woman to speak in a man's voice. They all burst out laughing;.

"Well done, good for you, let's go," Michael said, half in earnest.

Padraig continued to pose. "My new mantra in life is let's roll, let's rock, let's get some cock."

It was after midnight when they finally arrived at Buzzbees, the huge gay club down in Tottenham Court Road. On the way, the strange, fleeting looks of other passengers on the tube had only made Padraig more defiant as he re-applied his lipstick at every opportunity. The massive dance floor was crowded and in semi-darkness as the music blared and buzzed in their ears. The dry-ice machine nearly blinded them, but no one complained; the Subterranean on a Friday night now seemed a million miles away.

"We're children of the night," Michael shouted to each one of them as they all looked around in awe.

"Let's go get ourselves an adventure," Padraig screamed as he ran to the dance floor, followed by the others.

Alan immediately began to eye a dark-tanned man who looked like he was from the Middle East. "Wish me luck," he whispered to Cormac as he moved in. "Guess I'm off to see the one eyed camel."

The rest of them danced together for a while but within a half hour most had gone their own ways. Padraig had made contact with a burly builder type and headed off to the dark room at the back of the club. Michael was busy at the bar lashing in as much drink as he could get his hands on.

Siobhan checked her watch and said to Cormac, "Let's go, we can make the night bus if we leave now." Together they headed for the night bus and Hangman's Alley.

One of the barmen came up to Michael. "What time is it?" he asked. Michael, dazed, told him he didn't have a watch.

"It's time for action", the barman laughed. "I finish at two, wait for me." With that, a free double vodka was placed on the bar. Michael knew he was sorted for the night.

"POST'S ARRIVED," Alan exclaimed with a big laugh, calling to Cormac in the kitchen to come and have a look at the letters just dropped through the mailbox into the stark hall. Cormac stood in his fleece pyjamas, two jumpers and anorak as Alan handed him an envelope.

"Told you it would be no problem," Alan said enthusiastically, filling a saucepan with water to boil on the small two-ringed gas stove for tea. Cormac ripped open the envelope to confirm it was the Giro, which he could cash at the post office.

"My other Giro should be downstairs at the lads' flat," Alan said. "I must check it later"

"Does it not bother you?" Cormac asked. "Are you not afraid you'll be caught. Signing on twice is an offence. What if they come after you?"

Alan just laughed it off as he put on some toast under the grill. "It's nothing to me, sweetie, it's nothing to me. Don't worry about it."

"The only problem with telling lies is you have to remember an awful lot of things," Cormac threw in. "I suppose I should ring home now that I have a few bob," he added, sounding guilty. "But she does my head in crying every time I ring. At least she's still sending that tenner every week. Better keep her sweet."

Four weeks had passed, and it had become apparent that neither Alan nor Cormac were fond of work. Cormac had tried a job in a bar that Michael had got for him near the college. But it was hard work over long hours, and so he quit after three weeks, thinking could survive on the £55 every two weeks from the Giro and the tenner his mother sent him every week in the middle of the Dunglass Independent. Alan hadn't even tried to get a job, and decided to chance his hand at scamming by signing on twice, once in his own name and the second time in his cousin's name, Christopher, giving Michael's address on the ground floor. So far, so good, and Alan was pleased with his brilliant idea of getting his cousin to send him his birth certificate. He and Cormac could now stay in bed or lounge around until the rest of the gang came home in the evening. Then the clubbing could begin.

Their flat was bare, their only real protection against the cold being their coats and the blankets they had bought in Oxfam to cover them in their bedrooms. They spent most of their time downstairs in the others' flat. Cooking was a rare event. Money had to be saved for the night bus and flagons of cider.

"I think we should go out and get some supplies," Alan said with a big grin as he gazed at the Giro.

Cormac checked his watch. "Guess we'll get Harry before he finishes the stall."

"C'mon then, drink that tea and eat the toast fast, let's go and get him before he closes up." After making some investigations locally, Alan had found a new best friend in Harry, the veg man in the market, who would give you two apples and a fiver's worth of hash in the same bag. Harry Head, as they called him, could always be relied on for great gear.

MICHAEL PEDALLED as fast as his legs would allow on the old butcher's bike he had found in a skip. He had only ten minutes to get to the dole office to sign on. His life had become a series of hustles. Siobhan had remarked earlier in the morning that it was obviously signing-on day when she looked at Michael's clothes – his worn jumper and dowdy cords were his signing-on uniform. After locking his bike outside to the railings he took his place in the queue. It wasn't as long as usual and within twenty minutes he had signed on and was off to the Job Centre for his appointment with Mrs Cambridge, a pleasant, woman he had met her a couple of times before.

"Hello again, Michael, " Mrs Cambridge said as she signalled Michael to take a seat. "I see from your file here you've applied for lots of jobs." Michael nodded, putting on what he hoped would be an Oscar-winning face.

"Well, with the depression thing, I've been on these tablets," he said, throwing her an eye as he lowered his head. "I feel I'm just not able to cope sometimes."

Mrs Cambridge looked up from her file over her glasses with an encouraging smile.

"Well if you took a bit of pride in your personal appearance, Michael, maybe you could get out there and earn a living. Think about it. It's just that sometimes when we sit at home thinking so much we get depressed and too much into ourselves." She gave Michael a motherly smile. "The best thing you could do is keep looking at the board and keep applying for those jobs. There's one there for everybody. There is something there for you Michael."

He couldn't, of course, dare mention that he already had a job in the gay bar on Tottenham Court Road. With her speech of encouragement over and forms filled, Michael signed to register his attendance and then slowly made his way to the front door. When was he out of view of the Job Centre he broke into a run back to the dole office to collect his bike. Another fifteen minute sprint on the bike and he was back at college.

"Where have you been, Mr Duffy?" the lecturer sniped as Michael entered the classroom. Mr Floyd, who lectured in product design, had taken a dislike to Michael from the start and was always quick to pull him up. He stood staring at Michael who was slightly startled for a moment but gathered himself. He clicked into actor mode, looking sadder than before, eyes to the floor, heart in mouth.

"I ate some bad fish last night, Mr Floyd, and I've spent the last half an hour in the toilet, I'm very sorry I'm late."

"Okay, well just get to the bottom of the class and get into it. Ask Wigan there what the project is." Mr Floyd turned away with a bored sigh.

"Hustle, baby, hustle is the name of the game," Michael whispered to Wigan, his Rastafarian friend and fellow-student. He felt relieved that it would be two whole weeks before he had to sign on again.

IT WAS nearly six thirty by the time Michael arrived at the squat, where the smell of cooking hit him at the front door. He was greeted in the kitchen by Siobhan who had made a huge pot of stew.

Padraig came in not long after, and the three of them sat at the small kitchen table, the only communal room in the flat. Siobhan and Padraig had a bedroom each and Michael's room was the sitting room, which had a hatch from the kitchen. The gas and electricity were connected but, as Michael had warned them, squatting was always on a day-to-day basis.

"How's everything at college, Michael," Siobhan asked. She was always interested in what Michael was doing.

"It's hard, Siobhan," Michael said in a tired voice. "It's full of teaching staff who are semi-retired shop-floor manager types. They've landed themselves these cushy teaching numbers to teach a load of wogs and queers how to make shoes."

"You can't say things like that, Michael," Siobhan said. "Wogs and queers, you're not allowed."

"I'm in my squat, so I can say what I like," Michael snapped and was sorry immediately. "I'm sorry Siobhan, you're right. It's just that it's three thousand sterling a piece for these foreign students, most of them from Africa and Asia, and it is one of the few places that teaches shoe design so it does well out of it. I really do love what I'm studying, and there is amazing stuff going on in the college, but I hate the teachers and the environment is strange. There's a funny feeling to the place."

"How come we're having bread and butter with the stew?" Padraig asked.

"My father always had it that way," Siobhan said. "He was

from Mayo, and I always did it after my mother died."

"It tastes amazing," Padraig said, "amazing."

There was a knock on the front door. "I suppose it's the lads, they smelled your food," Padraig said to Siobhan as she got up to let Cormac and Alan in.

"Why is your place always warm and cosy and so full of nice things?" Alan asked as he came into the kitchen.

"It's because we spend money," Padraig said. "On other things beside hash."

"Why don't you go down to Oxfam," Siobhan said, "and get some second-hand furniture like we did, as well as pots and pans and do a bit of your own cooking?"

"But the lift, it's not working," Cormac replied with an immediate excuse.

"But you're only four floors up," Michael said. "You could carry the stuff up like everyone else." Siobhan was already dishing out two small bowls of stew and placing them on the table.

"How are you getting on at the gym, Siobhan?" Michael asked.

"I never knew it, but Hackney is the poorest borough in England, so seemingly Margaret Thatcher has given new money for the area to be regenerated. That's how they can open up Andrews Boxing Club again. It's run by this ex-soldier, Walter. He's an older nice man, real army type. But some of the men who come in, I swear, and the women, they train most nights, and you'd want to see the bodies on them, the muscles, amazing." Siobhan's eyes lit up when she spoke about fitness, muscles or anything to do with keeping fit. The martial art classes she had completed at home had stood to her in getting the job. "There's nothing really for the kids to do around this area, so I suppose the local boxing club gives them a focus. It helps rather than hanging around getting involved in drugs and gangs."

"How is Denise doing this week?" Cormac asked Padraig about

his boss. "Who's the latest man? Is he an Egyptian this time as well?"

"We had an Omar Sharif look-alike in yesterday, and he and Denise went out to the back room. All we could hear were giggles and laughs." Now that Padraig had all their attention and was centre stage, he threw in his new snippet of information. "According to Denise, Middle Eastern men, especially Egyptians, all shave their bodies from the tip of their toes right to their head." He stopped and stared, waiting for the reaction to his announcement.

"Every part?" Alan asked through a mouthful of stew.

"Every part," Padraig said, emphasising the words. Enjoying the attention, he delivered the punch line with perfect timing. "Apparently the one-eyed monster looks huge when it's hairless, and better still, they are all hung like camels, not donkeys but camels." They all nearly choked on their stew with laughter.

"IT'S AMAZING, the classes are going so well, never thought there'd be so many men who wanted to know about women's make-up," Padraig said as he and Michael were sipping a breakfast cup of tea in the squat.

Michael looked up from the letter he was reading.

"That's great, Padraig, I'm thrilled for you. Making the move was the hardest bit. Now that we're here in London, I know it's going to open up new doors for us both." Michael was always full of encouragement, trying to reassure himself as well as Padraig. "I have a letter from Pearl in New York. Remember I told you about her? She's coming at Christmas, says here she'll stay with Karen upstairs and she's starting her new writing course in January."

He turned his attention again to Padraig and his make-up course. "You're doing something you love and you're good at it. Bet you could make a career out of being a make-over stylist."

"Yeah, can you imagine if they could see me now back in Dunglass teaching men how to become women? Drag queens, cross-dressers, transvestites, or whatever label they could think of. Everything has to have a label in Dunglass."

"Forget about Dunglass and just concentrate on being here."

"It's hard to forget Dunglass. My dad rang the salon yesterday."

Michael was surprised at this news. "Is everything all right? How come he rang the salon?"

"Turns out he got the number from Martha, but the news is Bridie has cancer," Padraig said as if he was reading an announcement from a newspaper with no emotion in his voice. Michael knew Padraig's stepmother was a young enough woman in her early fifties.

"What did your dad actually say?"

"Seamus was full of medical information. It's breast cancer and apparently it's gone all through her. Shouldn't be long." Padraig's flippant attitude shocked Michael.

"Oh my God, that's terrible. What about Susan and Martha and your dad, they must be all devastated."

"Well, I suppose at this stage he's used to burying wives," Padraig said in a defiant voice. "At least he won't have to pay for another plot in the cemetery." He sipped his tea and added, "I wonder will he put her down on top of my mother?" For a few moments an awkward silence hung between them. Michael knew Padraig's coldness was a way of coping.

Eventually he said, "I hope you didn't say that to your dad."

"Of course I didn't, Michael, I'm not that bad. It's what I thought but I didn't say it."

"Thank God for that. Is she having treatment?"

"That's the whole thing, seemingly the treatment is over, they've done all they can and it's just a matter of time. Six to twelve months max."

"Are you going to go home then? I heard Alan and Cormac talking about going home for Christmas. You could go home with them if not beforehand."

"I am not. That woman has hated me all my life. She married my father but never wanted his baggage, me and Martha. She's treated us like second class citizens. So no I won't be going home to see her." There was bitterness in Padraig's voice.

"So what did you do when you got the news?"

"God forgive me, I took advantage of the situation, finished work early. Told Denise I was upset but in actual fact I got the tube down to the West End, found the first man that looked at me and had sex with him in the toilets. There, I've said it, Michael. What do you think? Does that mean I'm a sex maniac? Anytime I'm hassled, all I want to do is have sex."

"I'm no psychiatrist but you could lay off sex for a bit. You're going at it a lot lately. Maybe you should just take up boxing in Siobhan's gym, or think of some other way of relieving your stress." They giggled together. Padraig knew Michael was right. Since they came to London a few months back he had never had so much sex. Never in his wildest dreams had he imagined it possible to find so many men wanting casual encounters. It was thrilling, and he was enjoying every minute of it, but he had to admit that it also gave him a sense of uneasiness.

"Listen, I have to go, my class is in an hour," Michael said, getting up from the table. "Why don't you come down to the college later on or what's your plan?"

"The class is tonight and I promised everyone we'd go clubbing to Wonderland." Padraig paused. "I heard it holds three thousand people. You're welcome to join us after your shift in the pub, you know that goes without saying."

"Think I'll pass on that one," Michael said. "I've no problem with you dressing up but I'd say I'd look a bit strange in my Doc

109

Martin boots, jeans and tight haircut among all you ladies of the night, or whatever you call yourselves."

After Michael left, Padraig felt a wave of sadness come over him, but distracted himself by focussing on the new full-length velvet pink number that he had bought for the rendezvous with his class. He headed to the bathroom to shave every hair off his body from the tip of his toe to his chest.

MICHAEL'S HEAD was buzzing with excitement as he knocked on the door of Karen's flat. So many things were happening all at once. Pearl was sprawled out on the sofa but immediately jumped up and threw herself into Michael's arms.

"How are you, Michael?"

"I'm great, all the better for seeing you. Miss Pearl," Michael said, fondly looking at his friend.

"I'll leave you to it," Karen said. "I'm heading out for a bit."

"Mind the hoodies on the corner," Michael said. "They look stoned or drunk." They all knew at this stage to be careful of the gang of youths who gathered on the corner of the flats. As they went into the kitchen Pearl put on the kettle to make coffee and the friends caught up on all their news.

"I've a few weeks, Michael, before the writing course starts so I'm hoping to get a job, part-time or something, in the meantime. Maybe you could point me in the right direction."

"I'm sure we can find something for you," he said, then turned to what had been on his mind for a while. "How's Ernie doing?" he asked.

"He's now up in Woodstock, about two hours drive north of New York," Pearl said. "That bad cold he had turned out to be something worse. I went up on the bus once to see him. It's mostly a hospice for men who are HIV positive or are dying of Aids."

110

"That's terrible," Michael said. "So you don't know how long he's got?"

"That's the thing about this Aids flu, Michael, it seems to be a very painful lingering disease so they don't know how long, but at least he has someone to look after him. It's really sad isn't it?"

"It's terrible," Michael said quite shocked at the thought of Glam Ernie, a.k.a. Audrey Hepburn, in all his finery, now suffering a horrible disease that would definitely kill him. They sipped their coffee in silence, both unsure what to say.

"I heard something fascinating in college today,"Michael said eventually. "There's this bursary which I was thinking of applying for after Christmas. It's a competition where the winner gets to go to Milan in Italy for a year to learn how to design shoes." Michael's eyes widened just talking about it.

"Oh, that would be amazing," Pearl said. "You've got to apply."

They chatted a while more, Michael throwing around ideas about what type of project he would enter for the bursary until he noticed that Pearl's jet-lag was beginning to set in and that she looked shattered. "Listen I'll leave you," he said, "and I'll come back later or in the morning when you have had time to rest. I can introduce you to all the gang downstairs. Do you plan to stay here?"

"Yeah, Karen and Tom were looking for another lodger, so it's perfect really. I'm sorry, Michael, I'm not much company at the minute. We'll have lots of time to catch up, and I'm just thrilled."

Michael gave her a hug and left her to recover from her jet-lag. He made his way down the two flights of stairs to the ground floor and as he turned the key in the front door of the flat the smell of very strong hash hit his nostrils hard. Very quietly he unlocked the door of the sitting room, which was his bedroom. Alan and Cormac were sprawled on his bed, both clearly stoned out of their heads. They had climbed in through the hatch from the kitchen.

"Hi, Michael," Alan said. "Could you go on your bike to the Chinese and get us some fish and chips or better still spring rolls? Go on please, I'm starving."

"We've got the munchies, Michael, you know how it is," Cormac said. "If my mother was here now she'd feed us, no problem." At the thought of his mother, he began to cry.

"I'm no one's mother," Michael screamed. "Get your arses out of here." Alan began to laugh hysterically.

"I got my weekly Dunglass Independent today, Michael, with the usual ten pound note stuck in the middle. She really loves me so much."

Cormac was now bawling his eyes out. Michael looked at him with pity, a pathetic figure whose mother's apron strings stretched across the Irish Sea.

"Enough is enough, get out." Michael's patience was frazzled. "I told you this is not a drop-in centre and I am not a charitable institution. Out now!"

The laughing and crying continued as they staggered to their feet.

"Smoke all you want in your own flat but not in here," Michael said as he held the front door open for them.

Alan stopped for a moment at the threshold. "I was talking to Harry at the stall in the market . . .

"The one you got the hash off?" Michael said angrily.

"Well, we discussed other people's tribes and other people's lives. I feel really at one with black people and I love Bob Marley, so I really think that the anthropology course in the college would suit me down to the ground."

"Out now!" Michael barked again. He had heard enough over the past weeks of Alan's ramblings about doing an anthropology course. He eased the two of them out onto the communal landing and slammed the door shut. He headed back to his bedroom and opened the window as far as he could to let the smell of the hash out. If Alan and Cormac wanted to waste their lives away as two stoners, that was their business. He had other plans, and Milan was one of them.

"AND THEN the police came and they did their best to control the crowd, or mob I should call them." Padraig was explaining to Michael what had happened the night before just as the waitress in Al's Kitchen put the food down in front of them. "Me and the others eventually got out the fire escape exit at the back. It was very violent, Michael. I was afraid of my life."

"Why do English people always have beans for breakfast?" Michael said as he tucked into the huge breakfast in front of him. "They just make you fart."

"You're not listening to me, Michael."

"I am. Sorry, I'm sure you were afraid," Michael said, trying to picture the scene. Declan's shop had been surrounded by a mob while Padraig was in the middle of one of his classes.

"It was the Christian Brotherhood or the National Front. Declan's not sure, but he got anonymous mail before from one of them. They say it's immoral encouraging men to dress up as women, but last night it got very nasty. Only consolation is I got all the handbags."

Michael's ears pricked up at the mention of handbags. "What handbags?" he asked.

"The ones belonging to the people in my class which they left behind in the panic. Some of them are amazing. I'll have to show them to you."

"Bet you've been through all the personal stuff inside already," Michael said, looking directly into Padraig's eyes.

"Who, me? Never," Padraig laughed. "Of course I went

through every single one of them. And there was plenty of interesting stuff there."

"I'm sure you'll hand them back."

Padraig stalled as he made a sausage sandwich.

"Of course I will," he said. "They'll be delighted to get their handbags back, but I might keep a few of the personal things inside, just to hold on to in case."

"In case of what?"

"Just in case, for the future. I saw some of their personal cards with phone numbers and addresses. One's a politician, another one works for the BBC and another one is a judge."

"A judge?" Michael was shocked. "Which one?"

"Alistair, the one with the funny glasses."

Michael remembered Alistair's face from the first class, when he had gone along to give Padraig support.

"Turns out he's some big judge or barrister or something legal according to his card," Padraig said. "But the one that's most interesting to me is Tony, who turns out to be a big executive in the BBC.

"The one with the big nose?" Michael asked.

"Yeah, that's him."

"Oh my God, that's amazing. Maybe he could open doors for you, especially if you had information on him," Michael said sarcastically.

"Well, now that you mention it," Padraig said with a grin, "it did cross my mind. I might hold onto his card for future security."

"Are we talking blackmail here?" Michael said in a whisper.

"Don't give me that look, Michael. What are you, some kind of altar boy? I didn't mention the word blackmail, but who knows what the future might hold? It's just another option."

"Well, whatever way it goes you're on to a winner. They love you at the classes, you'll have more when Declan starts them up again and you could always write a best seller about the secrets of a drag make-up artist or secrets of a cross-dresser." Michael finished his breakfast. It was harmless banter between two friends, but Padraig knew deep in his mind that some seeds had been sown for the future.

CHRISTMAS DAY, LONDON

"YOU'RE A good boy, James. Look after Mam for me." Michael felt sad speaking down the phone to his younger brother.

"I'll pass you on to Mam, okay bye, Michael." Their mother came on the phone.

"I told you that Rita got engaged, didn't I Michael?"

"Yes, Mam, you did, and that dad is not there, he's working, triple time on a Christmas day." Michael tried not to sound impatient. "I hope you have a nice Christmas day, Mam." He was anxious to finish the call.

"We'll do our best," she said in a monotone voice. "It's a pity you couldn't come home, Michael, but, as you say, you have to work extra shifts. Have you any of your friends with you today?"

"Yeah, there's a group of us, Mam. We're going to have our Christmas dinner shortly, so just ringing you before we get started on the grub."

"Okay then, Michael." Her voice sounded distant.

"The pips are going, Mam, talk to you soon, bye." Michael put down the phone. He had another couple of quid in coins in his hand but a few minutes' call to home was all he could take. James's youthful enthusiasm always came across in his voice as he plied him with questions about London and college, but Michael always felt discouraged by his mother's lack of interest; she had never acknowledged his course in London.

115

Pearl was waiting for him outside the red telephone box, and together they made their way towards the flats.

"How are all in Cork?" Michael asked, imitating a Cork accent. Pearl had made a call home directly before Michael.

"Same old, same old" Pearl said flatly. "They're all in my mother's, my sisters, the kids, the gang. It's only twelve o'clock and I can hear from my mother's slurred voice she's pissed already. Nothing changes."

"Let's not worry about this today. Today is a happy day, no work, lots of food, lots of beer, lots of laughs, we're free."

The smell of the roast chicken and roast potatoes greeted them in the hall of Karen's flat. Tom, Padraig and Siobhan were busy organising the drinks and setting the table. Christmas music was playing in the background, and beer, wine, cider, gin and vodka were all lined up on the sideboard. The black and white television in the corner, now showing "It's a Wonderful Life" with James Stewart, was just one of the many items Tom had picked up from various building sites. The flat was warm and cosy as Siobhan passed around the huge box of Quality Street she'd received as a gift in the gym.

"Here's to little old Ireland." Padraig made the first toast of many that day. Fleeting thoughts of home transported him back to Dunglass, but immediately he poured another drink to help numb the loneliness and strange feeling of resentment.

The day flew by as they sat around the table, eating, drinking and chatting, later teasing each other unmercifully as they played Monopoly, which Michael had bought for the day in a second-hand shop. That evening, two friends of Tom's arrived laden with cans of beer, reinforcements for the night, and they all joined in a game of poker. Paddy and Jack, who were brickies from Dublin and lived in a boarding house in Kilburn, were too experienced as card payers for everyone else and took all of

116

Michael, Padraig and Siobhan's money. Drunk and broke, but happy, Siobhan and Padraig helped Michael down the two flights of stairs to their own flat.

"That's the first of many," Michael announced in a slurred voice when they reached the front door.

"The first of many what?" Siobhan asked.

"Happy Christmases away from Dunglass." Michael started giggling uncontrollably.

"Hear, hear" Padraig said. "I'm off to bed." He stumbled towards his room, bumping into the wall before he reached the door.

CHRISTMAS DAY, DUNGLASS

"I THINK I'll have a little doze, love, I'm exhausted. You don't mind if I have a little nap for ten minutes. Will you be able to look after yourself?" Cormac's mother looked over at him from her chair. She had completely smothered him with attention, looking after his every need, since he had arrived back home. He was almost embarrassed by it all. She closed her eyes and fell quickly asleep. Cormac stared at his father who was snoring in the armchair as another film was starting on the television. Creeping into the hall, he slipped on his heavy coat and headed into the cold night air towards the graveyard. Like old times, he thought, as the taxi pulled up beside him. As the car moved away from the kerb Cormac turned in the front seat to gaze at Pearse, a warm, fuzzy feeling hitting his tummy.

"I was looking forward to seeing you all day," he said.

"Yeah, me too," Pearse mumbled, not taking his eyes off the road. But with a smile and a touch of his hand on Cormac's thigh, he knew how to keep this younger man sweet until he got what he wanted from him. It had been on his mind all day. "Think we better chance the car tonight, the mobile home might be too cold," he said. "I know the perfect laneway right out in the country." Pearse put his foot down on the accelerator.

SPRAWLED ON the sofa, Alan had a clear view of his sleeping father on one armchair, mouth open and dribbling, a glass of whiskey still in his hand, while his mother collapsed from exhaustion with her knees wide apart on another chair. He felt revulsion at the sight of both of them

"Why is there a funny smell off Uncle Alan's cigarettes, Mam?" six-year-old Thomas, his sister's son, asked.

"Why don't you ask Uncle Alan?" Regina said in a spiteful voice. A recent separation from her husband had brought her back with her two children to her parents' home. They were a source of constant irritation to Alan since his return from London. The six-year-old's innocent question had jolted his granny awake.

"What do you mean, Thomas, I don't smell anything funny?"

"Don't mind him, Mother," Alan said, darting a look at Regina. "It's okay, English fags always smell different than Irish ones." Regina smirked and smiled as she moved towards the kitchen to refill her large glass full of vodka.

"What day are you heading back anyway? Shouldn't you be going soon, Alan?" Regina said as she passed him.

"Here's your hat, where's your hurry. It's only Christmas day, Regina. I've no intention of leaving anywhere at the moment."

"Now, now, kids, no fighting, not on Christmas Day," their mother said. "Let's just relax and enjoy ourselves. We don't want to be upsetting your father." Alan's mother was always the peacemaker. "Why don't you and Regina make the sandwiches together like you always do for the cards night?"

"What cards night?" Alan said out loud.

"The cards night, love, how could you forget?"

In a flash he remembered. The whole family always came every Christmas night and played cards on the kitchen table well into the early hours. The annual poker night. It was too much for him to take.

"I won't be here, Mother, I've got to go." Alan suddenly found the energy to jump up and leave the sitting room.

"Where are you off to, Alan?" His mother's face was covered with disappointment.

"I'm heading down to see Mary Rose, see what her plans are. I'm dying to see her engagement ring."

Leaving the house muffled up for the cold, Alan made his way to a caravan parked on the edge of town. He was taking the advice of the young teenagers he had talked to at the chip shop the previous night, who told him where he could buy the best gear in town.

LONDON 1987

"DO YOU know today is called Black Monday?" Siobhan asked as she and Padraig sat on the bed watching Michael lay out sketches for his project on the floor. The gas heater mounted on the wall was at full blast as Padraig asked lazily, "What do you mean, Black Monday?"

"Today is the day when credit card bills go out to those who use them over the Christmas, so today is a reality check and deep depression sets in. Well, so they were saying in the gym today."

"Just as well none of us have a credit card," Padraig sighed. The reality of living in London had hit all three of them, and the novelty was wearing off. Although the city brought freedom, it also brought a struggle for survival.

"I can't believe Finnuala's gone nursing in Liverpool," Michael said absent-mindedly as he laid out all twenty of his sketches in front of him. "She never seemed interested in nursing, and I thought she was all geared up for the civil service. Pity we don't have her address or a contact number, but my mother didn't have any of that information when I spoke to her last time on the phone, just the usual strained conversation."

"Join the club," Siobhan said. "My dad was close to tears, trying to lay the guilt on thick and heavy. The usual emotional blackmail story. We miss you, come home."

"At least I don't have any of that," Padraig contributed. "I spoke to my sister Martha the day before Christmas Eve in my aunty's. Leave them at it; they're welcome to Dunglass."

Michael was only half-listening to the conversation in the background. He was a man on a mission. Over the past few months in London he had watched people as if he was studying psychology instead of shoes, and had figured out why people bought fashion and designer labels.

"You know, it's a lifestyle," he announced out of the blue. Neither of them understood a word he was saying, their minds were still in Dunglass.

"What are you on about?" Padraig asked.

"The lifestyle choice, that's what the consumer is buying. The unfortunate punter who buys the label, that is the expensive shoes or coat or handbag, thinks that they will have a nicer life once they purchase these items." Siobhan and Padraig looked at each other just nodding and smiling, acknowledging that Michael was on his shoe designer trip again.

"There are two sides of the fence, the rich and the poor, and I've decided which side I'm going for," Michael said. Standing up, he stared down at his sketches to consider the final touches for the bursary award. He had three more weeks to get his project

120

together, and things were coming along nicely.

"What's your theme, Michael, what's it called?" Siobhan asked.

Michael was thrilled by her interest. "It's called 'Soul to Sole'."

"Maybe you would explain that to us mere plebs," Padraig said.

"I had this idea, you know when we were kids and we were forced to go to Mass? Well, I can remember sitting there, I must have been only about nine, and I was always amazed at people's shoes in Dunglass. I'd watch them go up to communion. It was like a fashion show. C'mon, do you not remember?" Michael looked from Siobhan to Padraig but neither of them had yet registered what he was talking about. He continued, "Do you remember the young ones there would watch the fellows, they'd wear their beautiful clothes and beautiful shoes as they went up to receive communion. It was like a catwalk. I reckon 'Soul to Sole' is a good theme to ask the question, is your soul more enriched by attending the church and talking to God, or your sole on your shoe because that makes a huge personal statement about your wealth and your status in the community."

"Oh my God, that sounds so deep and intense," Padraig said with the emphasis on intense. This was a joke between the three of them. If anything got too heavy, they dismissed it by saying, "It's too intense."

"Sounds good Michael," Siobhan said. "I like it, even if it is intense."

"Well I have to think of something different. At the end of the day, this competition is open to everyone in the UK. There will be hundreds if not thousands of applications, and there's an amazing prize. That's what I'm keeping in mind."

"What's the prize?" Siobhan asked.

"The prize is a whole year in a shoe college in Milan in Italy." Michael paused and watched their faces widen in surprise. "They give you the money to set yourself up in an apartment. Then you learn how to design shoes, cut patterns and get them made up in factories. Imagine a whole year in Italy. It's the heart of the world fashion industry." Michael's eyes lit up as he spoke.

"That's amazing, good for you, and go for it," Siobhan said. She got up from the bed and went to the kitchen. "Does anyone want a cup of tea?" she asked.

"Yeah, make a pot and we'll have a cup each" Padraig called after her. "I bought chocolate biscuits." On her return Siobhan poured from the old teapot from the Oxfam shop.

"Michael, do you know anything about this Section 28?" Siobhan asked. "I heard them talking about it today down the gym. Everyone's a bit afraid of it."

Padraig and Siobhan looked to Michael as a source of wisdom.. He always seemed to have all the inside information about the gay scene in London, much of it picked up in First Out.

"The manager in the bar has been living as an open gay man in London for most of his life, but he's afraid," Michael said. "That's why he got involved in local gay rights. Seemingly, Maggie Thatcher and her government have brought in this new law, Section 28. As far as I understand, it means that the government can't promote any material that shows people being gay or being homosexual. It claims it would be wrong for children to believe it's a normal thing to be gay. So anything that's already printed has been taken down in schools. It's now illegal to have information on gays on notice boards."

"That's a disgrace," Padraig said, then added with a giggle, "I was wondering why I got stranger looks than usual the last time I was dressed up as Shiel O'Blige on the bus."

"It's not funny, Padraig," Siobhan said "This really isn't good news. I could hear them talking about it in the gym okay. The crowd are mixed that are going to Las Vegas for the boxing competitions. There are men and women in that group, and I know some of them are gay. It's an unspoken subject, and now with this Section 28 it will be even more underground to be gay." Silence hung in the air. The implications of the new law began to dawn on Padraig.

"I hope this doesn't affect the new classes starting in Declan's shop next week. He told me he has twelve people lined up. If this gets out too much, it might frighten off the customers. I'll have to pop down to the shop in the next couple of days and talk to Declan. This is worse than being in Ireland."

"Stop that now," Michael said "At least it is still a big city, and you can come and go. I told you before to be on your guard, wear the Doc Martins and maybe you should put your wig away for a while, Padraig, until this blows over."

"What if it doesn't blow over?" Padraig was now getting concerned. "Didn't Pearl say that there's hysteria in America, that it's getting worse over there with this anti-gay movement and queer bashing. Isn't that why I left Ireland to come here and to be who I want to be?" His voice was becoming militant.

"Oh, will you shut up, I'm tired" Michael said. "Let's not get into a whole anti-Irish thing at the moment. All I know is you have to be careful now." He paused. "There's a strange vibe out there, an anti-gay vibe. It gives me a bad feeling, so just be on your guard."

"REGULATIONS, MR Duffy, regulations." Mr Floyd had a straight face but spoke with a smirking tone as he handed the file back to Michael. It contained his application form and project for the bursary award.

"What do you mean you won't stamp it?" Michael was shocked and his voice showed it. He was trying to contain the anger that was bubbling up inside him, anger that urged him to swing his right hand towards Mr Floyd's jaw.

"As I said the first time, no, we won't stamp it. You are only in second year, so technically it's impossible. You should read the application form again, Mr Duffy. It clearly states you have to be in third year to apply for this bursary." Michael

The subject was closed and he turned and walked out, leaving Michael standing in the empty classroom.

Michael tried to gather his thoughts. He knew that he would say or do something he would regret if he ran into Floyd again, so he decided to get out of the college as quickly as possible. In any case, he was due to start his shift soon at the bar. Grabbing his bike outside, and with his prized manilla file lodged close between his chest and his jacket, he cycled in a frenzy, his whole body seething with anger and resentment as he thought of Floyd's sneering face. What he needed most right now, he decided, was to get drunk, which he would definitely do after his shift was over, but in the meantime he would neck down a few vodkas or gins, or whatever he could get his hands on out of sight of his manager. He was aware he had been drinking more lately but consoled himself that it was understandable because of all he had to cope with: college, job, dole, squat, and now this ridiculous piece of college red tape that barred his way. Right now he was at a loss as to how he could cut through it, but deep down he knew there had to be another way.

MICHAEL STOOD outside the Royal Society of the Arts building on The Strand, his project in his hand together with a letter. He read it again for the umpteenth time, just to make sure everything in it was okay.

Royal Society for the Arts,
Bursary Awards,
The Strand,
London WSA 79.

8th February 1987

'Italian Shoe Project – Milan' – Bursary Awards 1987
Application 'Soul to Sole' by Michael Duffy, Wordwaines College,

Dear Judges,
Please judge my work as though I have received the college's
permission stamp. I am in my second year of the diploma course,
and it has been explained to me that I am therefore not yet eligible
to make this application. I would, however, like to make a special
plea that you at least consider my project as I believe that, in terms
of talent, I have the necessary qualifications to apply for the above
bursary. I have a passion for shoes and designing them, which I
think comes across in my project, and I urge you to give me the
chance of a lifetime by including me in this amazing competition.
The theme of my Project – 'Soul to Sole' – is based on my idea
when, as a small child of nine years old, I was brought to Mass
every Sunday. I was fascinated by people parading to Holy Com-
munion as if they were part of a fashion show. Their shoes told
so much about them as they knelt down to receive at the altar, and
as if on a 'catwalk' strutted back to their seats down the church.
While the 'Soul' is being enriched by attendance to church, the
'Sole' on their shoe made a huge personal statement of wealth and
status in their community.
Yours sincerely,
Michael Duffy

He replaced the letter in the large brown envelope that contained his project folder, sealed it and walked into the building. A pleasant woman at the reception desk took it from him with a smile and promised that she would pass it on. Outside, he unlocked his bike from the railings, happy that he had least done something, even if it was outside the regulations.

He made his way towards the coffee shop where he had arranged to meet Pearl. She had started her writing course and even though she was only upstairs in the flat with Karen and Tom, their lives had been so busy that they hadn't been able to see much of each other since that marvellous Christmas Day. She was waiting for him in the coffee shop, and they both hugged each other tightly. He always felt so much at ease with Pearl; it was always as if they just picked up where they had left off, even if they hadn't had a proper chat in weeks. He looked at her closely and immediately saw that she did not look too happy.

"What's on your mind?" he asked. "Is it home?"

"No, it's not home, Michael. I've been on the phone to my mother, and all is well. You know, the usual family stuff, mad drinking and family feuds. That's just the normal." Michael agreed with a laugh. "Then what's wrong?"

"I have something to tell you, Michael, and I don't think you're going to be very happy. I hate to be the one to say this but it's about Tom, Karen's boyfriend. With all that's going on now, he doesn't want you guys coming up to our flat anymore." Michael was gobsmacked. He stared at Pearl.

"It's because of these Aids ads on the telly isn't it, and this Section 28 bull that Thatcher has put about, isn't it?" he asked, knowing this was the answer.

"Yes, it is," Pearl said. "Anti-gay mass hysteria, I'm afraid. Tom is homophobic at the best of times. I know we had a good day Christmas day with his friends, but I guess he can't take too many

126

gay people all together. What, with you three and the two boys upstairs, I don't know. I'm sorry, but he doesn't want you calling to the flat any more."

"What is he afraid of, that he might get Aids from us when we use his toilet or drink tea out of his cups?" Michael asked bitterly.

"C'mon," Pearl said, taking Michael's hand. "Let's not get totally paranoid here but just keep away for a while anyway, cause no hassle."

"I've no intention of ever going up there again."

"Well, I can always pop down to you. We'll have to make appointments now to see each other." Pearl was doing her best to make light of the situation. "Anyway, did you put in the application?"

"Yes it's in, done and dusted. I've done all I can."

"Italy here we come," she said, toasting him with her cup of coffee. "To Italy."

"Yeah, to Italy" he said as he raised his cup of coffee towards her. "What about Ernie, how is he doing?"

"He's still in that hospital upstate," Pearl said. "He's not doing too well and has moved on to have fully fledged Aids now compared to HIV positive when he had the last blood test done. Also, I forgot to tell you the last time, he lost his job in the sex shop when his boss found out what was wrong with him. So I guess that there's mass hysteria about gay people on both sides of the Atlantic."

Michael took in what Pearl was saying and realised the seriousness of being "out". He promised himself that he would be a little bit more cautious in his behaviour, although of late he hadn't really had much sex as he was always too tired. By the time he got to a club he just drank too much and collapsed into a corner.

"You still sleeping in night clubs?" Pearl asked.

"Yes, it's my only saving grace. They say I could sleep on a postage stamp. Last week I fell asleep in Bojangles, woke up at three a.m. when the cleaners were in sweeping the floor. I guess exhaustion has kinda saved me from too much action lately."

IT HAD been an eventful day at the salon, Padraig recalled as he sat on the packed tube, avoiding eye contact with anyone. When he first started using the tube lines he had occasionally nodded to people but soon realised this was a no-no in London.

The words "grievous bodily harm" kept running around his mind. An hour after the salon opened, Nuala, the apprentice, had come rushing in the door, sobbing uncontrollably.

"What's wrong?" Denise asked immediately.

"I'm pregnant, that's what is wrong," she screamed, "and my boyfriend Wayne's been done for GBH."

"Inside again," Denise said as she threw her eyes to heaven.

"What does GBH mean?" Padraig remembered asking naively. Denise answered very flatly.

"Grievous bodily harm, last time it was just robbery." She gave a deadpan look to Padraig. The two women having their weekly perms were thrilled with all the gossip, just the thing to brighten up their day..

"Let's have a brew, darling." Denise nodded to Padraig to put on the kettle, but before turning he couldn't help asking, "Who did Wayne beat up?" Nuala's teenage pregnancy had paled into insignificance in Padraig's mind.

Nuala's voice softened as it always did when she spoke of Wayne. "Wayne was up at the local off-licence getting his cans as he does every day. These two queers were giggling and laughing and, worst of all, the owner served them first. Well, I can understand, Wayne just lost it." Nuala's innocent face stared at Padraig and Denise.

"How bad was it?" Denise asked.

"Oh, no, Wayne is okay, just a few scratches and bruises" Nuala automatically replied.

"I meant the poor men in the off-licence."

"Well," Nuala stalled slightly, "the police said one has a fractured skull and the other is still unconscious."

Padraig had spent the rest of the day looking after the customers, but his mind really wasn't on his work. He was deeply shocked that anyone could be so vicious to complete strangers simply because they were homosexual.

Joining the sea of people exiting at his next stop, he rode the escalator up to street level and strolled towards Declan's shop where he planned to have a coffee and talk about the new course that was due to start the following Wednesday. A dozen or more men were booked for the new batch of classes, including all five from the previous classes.

When he rounded the corner into the street where the shop was situated, he stopped for a moment in confusion, wondering if he had taken a wrong turn. But he knew he hadn't and when he looked down the street again he was gripped with panic. He began to run as fast as he could towards the shop. A fire brigade and two police cars were parked directly in front of the building. Grey smouldering smoke billowed through the broken main window and inside he could see the charred remains of the mannequins, and the boots and the shoes. A small crowd had gathered and the police had just finished securing a yellow tape in front of the shop out to street level.

"What happened?" a shocked Padraig asked two men, whom he recognised from the pizzeria just a few doors away..

"A fire, mate, early this morning, at four o'clock, they reckon," one of them said.

"The usual anti-queer gang were here late last night with their banners. Things got out of hand and the police were called. Apparently they left when the police asked them to, but some must have come back during the night and fire-bombed the place."

Ripples of fear shot up from Padraig's ankles and through his spine to his throat. He wasn't sure if he could speak.

"What about the owner, Declan," he finally managed to ask. "Did you hear anything?" He stopped breathing as he waited for the reply.

"Was taken out in a body-bag around lunch time. Died of smoke inhalation, we heard the cops say. That's why it's a crime scene now."

The blood drained from Padraig's face, and his legs felt unsteady as he staggered to the edge of the path and vomited between two parked cars.

"Are you okay, kid?" One of the men from the pizzeria came to stand beside him. "Here, take him inside." He beckoned to the other man and they both helped him inside the pizzeria.

"I'm sorry, I'm sorry, I'm okay," were the only words he could manage. "I'll be fine. Could I have a drink of water please?" His head was dizzy.

"Sorry about that, didn't know you knew the man," one of the men said. He offered Padraig a brandy, but he stuck to water and stayed for at least ten minutes drinking two glasses. Looking around him, he felt as if he was watching himself from the outside, a strange, surreal feeling. He needed to see Michael. Like a drunken man he fumbled through his pockets until he found a twenty pound note. He asked the staff to call him a taxi. He would head to the First Out, where he knew Michael was doing a shift.

"YOU'VE BEEN short-listed." Mr Floyd spat the words out at like bullets from a gun. Michael couldn't believe what he was hearing. There had been 370 applicants, and the short-list was down to five. The exhaustion of the past few weeks lifted from his shoulders.

"As I've told you before, Mr Duffy, you won't win," Mr Floyd said. Michael stood staring down at him as he sat behind his desk, while his colleague, Mr Kilbride, stood to the right with a blank expression on his face.

Michael stayed calm, suppressing the resentment he felt. "Thank you very much, sir," he said and turned to leave.

The news had ignited a new energy in him, which even the misty greyness of Hackney couldn't quash as he made his way home for a few hours' sleep before starting his shift in the bar. As he turned the key of the front door he heard voices from inside the kitchen and got a strong smell of hash. His heart sank as he realised that Alan and Cormac had taken refuge in the heat of the kitchen.

"Get this stuff out of here," Michael shouted as he waved his hands to dispel the smoke and went to open a window. The two others started to laugh.

"You know the gas is off in our squat," Alan said "We told you last week the council are on to us so we have no heating up there and its freezing."

Cormac, off in another zone, sat there with a stupid grin on his face.

"You could always look for another flat. There are lots of empty ones in the building. I told you before, why don't you get off your big fat arses and get another place?"

"Oh, stop it, Michael," Alan whinged. "You're so hard on us, we're doing no harm, we're just relaxing."

"Well you are not relaxing anymore in my flat, now get out." Michael put his hand under Cormac's elbow to lift him up. "Out!"

"Well, be like that then," Alan said.. "I was thinking of going home anyway."

Cormac suddenly came to life. "Yeah, we know the Social is after him," he said, referring to Alan.

"They're not quite after me, Cormac, so don't be such a drama queen" Alan said. "It's just that stupid social worker said she might pay me a house call, and I can't remember which address I gave her. I'm getting confused on numbers and outfits." Alan giggled again, thinking this was hilarious.

"Too much strong ganja affects the memory cells," Michael told them, but he knew he was wasting his breath. "Look, you can come out tonight. Padraig and the girls are coming down to the bar later. It's his first night out since the fire, so why don't you go sober up, change out of your signing-on outfits and come down later on."

"These are not our signing on outfits Michael, they're just the only clothes we had left that weren't dirty," Cormac said as Michael was closing the front door on them.

Michael headed to his room and threw himself on the bed, glad to forget his two friends and to have time to himself to savour fully the news he had got at the college. In his excitement he knew he would be on tenterhooks for the next few weeks until the winner was announced. Thoughts of Italy and all it had to offer ran around in his mind until he closed his eyes and drifted of to sleep.

IT WAS Friday night, and the First Out was packed to capacity. Michael came back upstairs from the cellar with a crate of bottles and started to refill the shelves. As usual, he had managed to drink half a bottle of vodka while he was down there alone. Niggling pangs of awareness made him realise that drink was beginning to have less effect on him.

His thoughts were interrupted by his colleague Graham telling him to watch the television. Looking up, he saw most people in the bar were staring at the black and white ad on the telly. It showed a man staggering down a dark corridor followed by a collage of lilies floating on the sea. It then showed shadows and icebergs appearing, spelling the word Aids like an evil spirit. These new ads were running daily now, orchestrated by Maggie Thatcher's government to highlight the spread of Aids. The press were having a field day, and Maggie Thatcher was being accused of being anti-gay, trying to rid the world of queers and drug addicts. As Michael gathered glasses from the tables he could hear people talking about the new dangers lurking for gay people, between the government's homophobic actions and the deadly Aids virus. On his way back to the bar his spirits were lifted as he saw Padraig and the others enter the bar. This was the first night Padraig was venturing down to the West End since Declan's death, and, at Michael's request, Siobhan and Pearl had brought him to the bar to have a few drinks on the way to the club. Alan and Cormac, who had managed to change their clothes and looked a bit more presentable, were in tow.

Michael dashed in behind the bar and served Siobhan five pints of cider, telling her to take Padraig and the others into the snug, where there was someone he would like them to meet.

A lone woman sat in the snug. Padraig, Siobhan and Pearl joined her at the table while Alan and Cormac sat on the small stools. "This is Christine, " Michael said. "She's a regular and one of our most glamorous customers"

"Another bottle of bubbly, darling," the husky voice requested.

"Coming right up," Michael said and headed back towards the bar. As Padraig sipped his cider, he stared across the table and then realised that Christine was in fact transgender, a real life transgender person. Oh my God, he thought to himself, this was a woman who had once been a man. He could see that she was a stunningly beautiful woman with high cheekbones and very expensive clothes. Judging by the length of her legs, which dangled out from her tight, short skirt, she must have been at least six-foot-two. Her blond hair and thin body gave her a willowy model figure. Padraig didn't dare to speak but wondered if the others had copped on. Within a few minutes Christine started to speak, a sombre mood overtaking her as she told them her life story.

"When I came to London first I saved up for the operation," she said as she lit up a cigarette. The others stopped their chit-chat between themselves, turned and faced Christine to listen to her every word. "I thought I'd find solace down here in London, thought I could be who I wanted to be, but I don't know, it's a crazy world. London's not quite as bad as Glasgow but this entire anti-gay thing, the marches, it's kind of frightening."

Cormac came to life and butted in. "What operation did you have?" Padraig sniggered to himself at Cormac's innocence and felt like saying something to his friend, but Christine was on a roll and he didn't want her interrupted any further.

"Well, it didn't take much surgery before a he became a she, and I got the chop," Christine said, pointing a long finger towards her genital area.

Cormac stood up flustered, his face a beetroot red. "I'll have to get some fags from the bar", he said as he grabbed his pint.

Alan, who had sneaked an extra-strong joint before leaving the squat, was imbued with an excessive confidence about his ability to be witty. "You mean you had the whole thing chopped off, there's no more 'how's it hanging,'" he said as he went into hysterics of laughter.

Padraig glared at his friend. "Will you shut up, Alan, sorry about that, Christine, go ahead. Don't mind him. He's just a dickhead." Christine nodded to Padraig in appreciation.

Michael came in to leave a bottle of champagne in front of Christine and hurried back out.

"Go on ahead," Pearl said. "What happened next when you got to London?"

"I remember one night I was drinking in a private club out in Kensington, minding my own business," Christine said, "not long after the operation. The manager came over and proposed that I 'service' some members of a French rugby team, five of them in all, who were staying nearby." She paused to let this much of her story sink in to their eager ears. Pearl's and Siobhan's mouths dropped open, and Padraig's eyes widened. Alan just giggled.

"Now even I was shocked because truly I didn't think they would really want me, and let's face it I didn't think I'd end up in the oldest profession in the world. But a girl's gotta do what a girl's gotta do." Padraig looked at her amazed

"So what did you do?" he asked.

"What did I do?" Christine shrugged her shoulders "I named my price in cash of course, ordered a bottle of the best champagne to be brought back to the room where I took on all five of them, one at a time." She took a sip of her champagne, poising to deliver her punch-line. "We all see what we want to see, and all they saw was a beautiful woman."

No one said a word, not even Alan, as they all sat mesmerised by her story. Padraig was about to ask something when a huge crash sounded throughout the bar.

"Queers, fags, weirdos, woofters," some men's voices screamed from outside, followed by the screeching sound of a car pulling away quickly. The large front window had been shattered by a cement block, and some of the customers had been hit by the flying glass. Michael and the other staff members helped the injured people until two ambulances arrived with the police. All the police and ambulance men wore disposable plastic gloves, which they now always did when entering a gay bar or club. After the ambulances left, the manager closed up the bar, and Michael left with the others to head back to Hackney on the night bus. The sight of the young teenagers burning a fire in a barrel at the corner of the flats made Michael and the others walk faster. It was only when they reached the inside of their squats that they finally felt safe.

IT WAS their first St Patrick's Day in London, so Padraig and Michael decided they would have a good pub crawl after taking part in a gay rights march in Hyde Park. Hundreds of people had turned up, many of them carrying banners that attacked Maggie Thatcher as a gay basher and demanded Section 28 to be withdrawn.

"I'm dying for a pint," Michael said when the march ended. As they began to move away, an announcement came from the podium that Freddie Mercury had been diagnosed with Aids. A shocked response rippled through the crowd.

"C'mon, I definitely need a drink now," Michael said and he led the way towards the West End, where they hit a bar they both knew. Two pints of beer with two whiskey chasers took the edge off Michael's jangling nerves and set Padraig quite tipsy.

The manager, whom Michael had met in First Out, came over to him. "I suppose you heard about Christine?" Michael stared blankly at him.

"Its touch and go, mate, they think she won't make it. She was set upon by a gang last Thursday night, she's on a life support machine" Michael and Padraig were stunned and took a seat in a quiet corner.

"Between Declan and now Christine," Padraig said shakily, "this queer bashing thing is getting out of control. I'd almost consider going home."

"Calm down Padraig, deep breath, relax. All we have to do is stay safe and make sure we all stick together. This will pass, it has to." Michael was saying the words but didn't really believe them. "Hiding out in Dunglass is not the answer."

Padraig spoke as if he were in a trance. "When I think about all the sex I've had with lots and lots of different men, I realise now that I took an awful lot of chances going home with strangers."

"Didn't we all, Padraig," Michael said. "I suppose if we didn't take the chance we'd never find love, but now it's 'No glove, no love.' I see they're handing out free condoms at all the marches."

"As if everyone is going to wear a condom each time they have sex," Padraig said.

"I don't know, Padraig." Michael looked directly at him. "It scares me because every time you have sex now you could catch this deadly disease. I get a very bad feeling about this. I think I need another drink."

As the day wore on they wandered around Soho, ending up in a pub called "Gangway". It was late in the evening and they were both quite drunk. Michael wanted to call it a night but Padraig insisted on staying for just one more.

"How's it going, mates," a deep Dublin accent asked them. Through his drunken haze Michael recognised Jack, Tom's friend who had joined them on Christmas day. Immediately he bought a round of drinks for the three of them, after which Michael knew he couldn't take any more and decided to head home. As he was leaving the pub was buzzing, and Jack and Padraig had joined in the Irish rebel songs being sung.

IT WAS six thirty next morning when Michael staggered to the toilet for a quick pee. As he turned his head he noticed parts of the bath were streaked with blood. Confused, he headed back to his bed but was stopped by the sound of crying from Padraig's room. Opening the door, he saw Padraig lying on the bed in a foetal position.

"What's wrong, what's happened, Padraig?" Michael asked.

"I was raped last night." Padraig was able only to whisper the words.

"Oh my God," Michael said and threw his arms around Padraig, who immediately flinched.

"Please, don't touch me," he said. Michael pulled back to stare at Padraig, who was white as a ghost.

"I'll make us some tea," were the only words that came to Michael's mind.

"Yeah, you do that," Padraig said. "Tea solves everything."

Michael tiptoed in to Siobhan's room and told her what had happened. They went back to Padraig's room and sat with him, encouraging him to tell them what had happened. Padraig was reluctant at first to say anything but then let the story out bit by bit.

He had stayed in the pub until closing time, after which he and Jack got the same bus. Jack had insisted that he wanted to make sure that Padraig got home safely, and came with him into the flat, which registered as strange to Padraig, but in his drunkenness he wasn't thinking straight. Jack then led Padraig towards his bedroom "like a rag doll" and closed the door behind them. He felt confused as he stood leaning inebriated against the door for support and saw Jack casually take off his shoes, jeans and underpants.

Padraig started to say something when Jack lunged at him and punched him hard in the stomach, so hard that he was afraid he wouldn't get his breath back. He had sobered up quickly in his mind, realising the danger he was in, but his body was still too anaesthetised to do anything. He tried to scream out, but Jack held his hand over his mouth and threw him on the bed. He then pulled down his jeans and underpants and attacked him from behind with brute force, causing Padraig immense pain. After he was finished, he laughed and threw him to one side, then casually stood up to put his clothes back on and left the flat without a backward glance.

After what seemed a very long time, he had managed to gather his strength and make his way to the bathroom where he vomited violently into the toilet and then had a hot bath to clean away the blood and the dirt he felt clinging to his body. He felt foolish and stupid to have trusted a fellow Irishman. Not for one moment had he thought of any romantic involvement.

"You have to go to the police, Padraig" Siobhan said.

Padraig moved to sit up in the bed.

"And what can the police do, let's get real," he spat. "I'm gay, I'm a homosexual man, lets face it they'll have no sympathy for me. They'll say I asked for it, so don't talk about police to me."

Michael went to the chemist and got some antiseptic cream and painkillers and was back in the flat within fifteen minutes. On his return, the three of them sat in silence for a while until finally Padraig spoke

"You know, I read about it before. Most rapists are people known to the victim. That's the shocking thing. I've heard it but I've never believed it."

He paused for a moment to think and then said in a whisper, "I feel so ashamed."

"Why don't I get you some strong gear from Alan, you can have a little smoke and you'll sleep," Michael said. "I'll ring Denise and tell her you're not well."

"That's a good idea," Siobhan said. "I'll stay here with Padraig, go on Michael go up to Alan, see what he's got or else go down the market. We can all have a chat this evening. Maybe things will be a bit clearer then about what to do."

Siobhan hoped she was right.

AFTER HE opened the front door, Michael told them to leave their luggage in the hall and guided them to the kitchen.

"Fresh tea and toast," Padraig said, pointing to the kitchen table. "Set you up for the journey ahead."

"That's very kind of you, Padraig," Cormac said, feeling guilty that he hadn't been able to talk to him since the vicious attack. Alan didn't say a word but immediately dived on the toast as if oblivious to everyone else.

"Well, are you all set lads?" Michael stood leaning against the door and let the three others sit on the only stools they had.

"Yeah, we've everything packed, getting the bus to Kings Cross, train to Holyhead and boat from there." Alan happily listed the journey ahead. Serious doubts had been running through his mind since his return from Ireland at Christmas. His decision had been helped by the daily reports of gay bashings and the horrible Aids ads on the telly, but the real clincher had come when Siobhan came up to their freezing flat and cried as she told them of Padraig's rape. "We booked one-way tickets when we got our Giro last week," Alan concluded.

"Be honest, Alan," Padraig said. "The fact your social worker was on to your case and you'd gotten your names mixed up on her two files didn't help the situation."

"At least I've given London a go," Alan said defensively, "and my mother and father need me."

Padraig handed two small parcels to Cormac. "Siobhan left a small parcel for her dad, and there's one there for Martha. If you don't want to call to the house I'm sure you could give it to her at Mass on Sunday."

Padraig tried to fake a smile. The tightness in his chest was particularly bad today, accompanied by the usual feeling of dread.

"Guess we'd better head," Alan announced as he stood up from the table, every piece of toast eaten. "I'll use the loo before

140

we go." Michael moved towards the hall and opened the front door, leaving Padraig and Cormac alone in the kitchen. The two of them made direct eye contact.

"I'm so sorry, Padraig," Cormac started. "Guess I'm a coward, didn't know how to handle it or what to say." Cormac observed the grey pallor of Padraig's face.

"There's nothing to say, well, nothing that anyone can say." Padraig's eyes were empty as he spoke. "It happens. It happened to me and I'm fine."

Not believing a single word, Cormac threw his arms around Padraig and hugged him tightly, holding back the urge to bawl his eyes out. No more words were spoken as Cormac quickly withdrew and headed towards the front door. Cormac placed his hold-all on his back and he moved ahead with Michael, strolling towards the front of the flats. Alan gathered his own bag and shook hands with Padraig before following them.

Michael whispered to Cormac. "You know he'll never leave his wife for you, don't you?" Cormac was taken aback, but knew Michael had his best interests at heart.

"Maybe you're right, Michael, but it's just too much like hard work here. After what's happened lately, maybe I'm just one for an easy life." They strolled down Hangman's Alley and arrived in a few minutes at the bus stop.

"Guess this is it, lads, you keep in touch," Michael said as he hugged both of them and without delay turned and walked slowly back to the flat.

The two friends sat silently beside each other on the bus, each lost in his own thoughts. Although Cormac felt deflated about giving up on London, he consoled himself by thinking of Pearse waiting for him at home. Alan had more practical thoughts – of how long it would take before he could score some gear as good as he had got at Christmas.

Alan broke the silence. "Think I'll fake a nervous breakdown in a few weeks. I heard them say that one night in the big red house and you're on the social welfare, the disability, for life." He was referring to the mental asylum five miles outside Dunglass.

"So that's your big plan for your financial future?" Cormac said. "If your sister Regina and the kids are still living in your mother's house you might stay there for more than one night." Cormac was getting fed up with his friend, who threw him a dirty look, ensuring that silence returned.

Not long after Alan and Cormac left, Padraig headed to work, having agreed with Denise that he would be a bit late that day. The nervous energy in the pit of his stomach had helped him to carry out his daily activities. He knew that, although he had become thinner, to others he appeared normal. Inside, however, he felt like an empty shell. Something deep within him had died, but as yet he was unsure of its name. Better not to trust any one ever, he decided, better not to speak about his feelings. He would cope with this alone.

"DO YOU think he's all right?" Siobhan asked Michael as they walked along the street together.

"I think he's getting there," Michael replied. They crossed the street, heading towards the post office on Caledonian Road.

"It makes me feel so helpless, but if he won't go to the police or the doctor . . ." Siobhan stopped mid-sentence, not sure what to say next. With her hold-all on her back, she was on the way to work.

"Look, I know we're both worried about him, we'll just have to keep an eye on him," Michael was firm. "Padraig is a survivor. Just give it a bit of time and we'll keep a close eye." Michael was worried about Padraig, but right now he was more preoccupied with a possible problem he might have to face himself. That morning, a note through his front door told him that a registered letter was waiting for him at the post office. Someone else at First Out had also received a registered letter from the social welfare services, informing him that he would have to attend the dole office for an interview; it looked like someone had ratted on him about working and drawing the dole at the same time. Michael expected the worst, and he wondered how he could handle the situation. His instinct was to ignore the letter, but he knew that would not solve the problem.

"Don't forget about the gym night," Siobhan said as they reached the post office.

Michael looked blankly at her. "Remind me," he said.

"Some of the men and women in the gym are training for this huge competition in Las Vegas in May, and they're having a charity night to help raise money for the flights." Siobhan's eyes were excited as she spoke. "You'd want to see them, Michael. They train like machines, like robots, you'll see them yourself. You're coming aren't you?"

"Sure, count me in," he said as Siobhan headed up the street. "See you later."

His stomach was in a knot as he entered the post office. A woman behind the counter took his passport to confirm his identity and then handed him the letter, which he took to a quiet corner and opened reluctantly.

He gasped. The words "won the competition" jumped off the page, and he realised also that in his nervousness he had not seen "College of Fashion" clearly printed on the envelope. He read the letter again slowly.

We are pleased to inform you that you have been awarded the Bursary for the Italian Shoe Project - Milan – 1987. Full details have been submitted to your college, Wordwaines College, London, which set out the travel dates and times when you must report to the Italian college. Please phone the number below to confirm your acceptance of this bursary, so that accommodation can be organised together with transfer of funds. Further information will follow pending receipt of your reply.

As he stood holding the letter, reading it again and again, Michael's chest was bursting with excitement. "Won the competition," he kept repeating over and over in his mind. He tucked the letter safely in his pocket and headed towards Denise's hair salon. Arriving outside, he could see Padraig at work through the window and realised that his friend was getting thinner and thinner all the time, but he pushed this thought aside and rushed in the door, shouting, "I've won, I've won."

He jumped up and down as he waved the letter in Padraig's face. "I've won, I've won." The woman having her hair blow-dried by Padraig looked startled.

"I've won, I've won, I've won." Michael was dancing around the salon.

"I do apologise," Padraig said to the woman, "it's just that we're Irish and we're both a bit crazy."

Denise emerged from the back room, and Michael handed her the letter.

"Imagine, Denise," Padraig said, bursting with pride, "three hundred and seventy five applications in the whole of Britain and my friend Michael wins it."

"This calls for a brew," Denise said, which saw Nuala automatically put on the kettle. She plied Michael with questions about the prize,

"It's a year in Italy," he could hear himself say, hardly believing it.

"Just think," Denise said slowly in a semi-trance, "of all those beautiful Italian men with their sallow skin. Oh, my God, I get weak at the knees thinking about them. She looked from Michael to Padraig as she said, "I suppose you'll be going with him?"

"Where?" asked a puzzled Padraig.

"To Italy. They need hairdressers there too, you know," she said, then added quickly, "Maybe I shouldn't be giving you such ideas. Don't want to lose my best stylist, but don't tell Nuala I said that." She winked at Padraig. "Why don't you finish early and go off and celebrate with Michael, have some fun, you deserve it. You're looking a bit peaky lately."

Denise looked directly at Padraig. She knew something bad had happened to him recently; he would confide in her when he was ready. Not having to be told twice, Padraig grabbed his coat and together he and Michael danced down the street like two children escaping from school. As they passed a red phone box, Michael said on impulse, "Have you any change Padraig? I'd love to tell my mother about the competition. C'mon, I'll try and call."

Michael pressed the button to drop the money into the coin box when he heard his mother answer in a timid voice.

"Hello, Mam, I've won the competition, the one in Italy I was telling you about," he said excitedly.

"Oh that's fine, that's very good, Michael," his mother said flatly.

"It's the whole of England, Mam, I've won the whole of England, and it means that I'll be going to Italy for a year."

"Oh, Italy now, is it? Oh, right, and when will that be?" Her tone was like a bucket of cold water poured over his excitement.

"Its July, Mam, but I'm going there in late June," Michael said, realising that he had been naive to think that her reaction would have been any different.

"Well, it's just that you know your sister's saving hard to get married, so keep that in mind," was all she could reply. Michael held the receiver away from his head and let his mother ramble for a minute about the wedding arrangements. The pip sounds signalled that his money had run out.

"Bye bye, Mam, bye Mam," he managed to say just before the line went dead. He left the phone box deflated and lit up a cigarette for himself and Padraig.

"Why don't we go for a few well-deserved pints before heading back to the flat?" Michael suggested. He had decided to banish the disappointment he felt from his mother's reaction.. "We can even go down the West End later, if you want."

"I think we'll stay local, if that's okay, Michael, let's not go too far afield." Padraig's sense of adventure had become dampened, and staying within easy reach of the flat had become the norm for him.

"Maybe Denise is right, you could come with me." Michael's stomach was doing flips with excitement at the thought of the two of them in Milan together. But looking at Padraig's sad eyes, he wasn't so sure that his friend was quite ready for such a drastic life change.

ALL SIXTEEN stone of the wrestler's bulging muscles landed on the floor of the boxing ring and covered the smaller frame of her opponent. Gasping sounds could be heard around the gym as the two opponents played to the large crowd.

"What's her name?" Padraig whispered to Siobhan, not able to take his eyes off the biggest woman he had ever seen.

"The big one's Natalie, she's amazing isn't she?" Siobhan gushed as she stared at the exposed flesh glistening with baby oil. "Look at the size of her arms and those thighs." Natalie had her opponent's leg in an arm lock and was pulling it backwards, causing her to moan loudly in pain.

"Please tell me that she's not really breaking your woman's leg," Padraig whispered again.

"It's all for show, Padraig, cop yourself on," Siobhan said. "She does a thousand skips of the skipping rope while she's warming up before she even gets into the ring. Well she wants to be a he, so she is saving up for the operation."

"Women can have operations too?" Padraig looked baffled. "But there's nothing to cut off," he added with his own logic.

"Let's just say they take these expensive tablets to make the lips bigger down there," Siobhan said in a whisper, moving her eyes down to her genital area and looking around to make sure no one was listening. "The lips grow longer and then the surgery sews it all together to make one big long lump." Pausing, she looked at Padraig and then down towards his groin. "Just like the one you take for granted." Padraig automatically moved his hands between his legs.

"That's too much information for me," Padraig said with a shudder.

"Natalie is from around here, but her parents are Greek. She's a bouncer in a club and does nixers when necessary." Siobhan had stalled on the word nixers.

"What do you mean, nixers?" Padraig asked. They stood on their feet and clapped as people gave the wrestlers a standing ovation.

"I hope the others get here soon or they'll miss all the fun, they're late," Siobhan said as she sat back down.

"What kind of nixers does she do?" Padraig repeated, a faint light bulb starting to flicker in his brain.

"I met her in the Lesbian Liberation Brigade. I told you about them, Padraig, but you never listen to me. Anyway, she is one of the leaders. She hates most men but is willing to suffer and do jobs if it means she'll get money to become one." Padraig looked even more confused, and Siobhan knew she would have to spell it out for him. "Like the gang that used to gather on the corner at the gym and jeer at us all when we were coming in and out, calling us queers, wogs, and weirdos. We got together, had a chat with Natalie. Herself and a couple of the girls on the committee moved in on the crowd with their bare hands. They haven't been at the corner since."

"Oh, right," Padraig said, watching Natalie at the far end of the gym as she spoke to the other wrestlers. "I'd like to meet her. Could I talk to her after the show?" Siobhan instinctively knew what was on Padraig's mind.

"Okay, I'll have a chat and see if you can meet her. Leave it with me."

Not long afterwards Michael and Pearl came and took the seats that Padraig had held for them. Together they watched the rest of the exhibition bouts of boxing and wrestling. The night finished with tea, coffee and biscuits as Siobhan buzzed around with excitement, thrilled at the success of the event she had helped organise.

"Not tonight," Siobhan whispered to Padraig, out of earshot of the others. "There are too many people around. She'll let me know a time that suits, very soon, and we can have a private chat with her." For the first time in many weeks Siobhan saw a spark of life in Padraig's eyes.

JUST STARTING his third pint of cider, Michael lit another cigarette.

"You're hitting it early today," he heard a voice say and looked up to see Pearl.

"I got you a coke, knew it would be too early for you," Michael said as he pulled out a stool for her from underneath the table. Both of them often met after college at the Hangman's Head on Camden High Street. The pub was quiet, with just a few day-time stragglers, the early evening lull before the night drinkers descended from the local flats.

"It's only five o'clock, Michael. You're drinking too much lately, you know that." Pearl was never afraid of speaking bluntly to her friend.

"Lay off, Pearl, you know I'm trying to steady my nerves. Any-way, read that." Michael handed Pearl the letter from the college informing him that he had failed his diploma. Continuing assess-ments by the teachers throughout the year contributed in part to the results of the final diploma. It was clear to Michael that they, and Floyd in particular, had taken a stand against him in reprisal for his winning the competition without their approval.

"But they can't do that." Pearl was shocked. "They have to give you the diploma. You've earned it. They have to give you a reason for failure, Michael, did you know that?"

"But I'm tired Pearl. I just feel knackered from it all." Michael took a big slug from his pint. "The teachers treat me like dirt, they totally ignore me in class. I heard Kilbride say to Floyd the other day in the corridor 'Look there's the queer paddy', and then they started giggling and laughing. It was like I was a piece of dirt on their shoe."

Lighting up another cigarette, he wished he had the money on him for a whiskey chaser but he had stopped carrying much around with him as a way of saving as much as he could for Italy.

"Look, Michael," Pearl said after a few moments, "we both know that people are now afraid of gays or anything to do with homosexuals. I know it and you know it. Those ads on the telly don't help. This means that the likes of Floyd and Kilbride are going to be everywhere, no matter where you go in the world.

It's just pure ignorance on their part and envy. They're stuck in that horrible college, but you're on your way to bigger and better things. If you didn't drink so much, even lay off it for a while, you could get your mind clear, do up a plan and go and talk to the students' union in your college." She sipped on her coke. "They can help you put together some kind of a letter and they'll fight for you. You can handle this, but just not on your own."

Michael listened as he finished his pint. He would like to have bought another but didn't want Pearl to go anymore about his drinking.

"That's a good idea, Pearl, will we head on home?" he asked.

Pearl gathered up her stuff and they headed out towards the bus stop. "I'm looking around for a new flat," she said. "I can't take Tom, he's so bigoted, and Karen's besotted with him. I heard there are some nice empty properties in Islington."

"Suppose you could move into our flat when I go," Michael said. "I've only a few more weeks left and my room will be empty. Mind you, we got a letter from the council during the week and I think the electricity might be cut off, so we bought lots of candles in the pound shop."

"Not a bad idea," Pearl said. As they saw the bus coming towards them Michael threw in, "We can get a few flagons of cider when we get off at the other end, save us hawking them on the bus." Pearl threw her eyes up to heaven, realising that Michael hadn't really taken on board all she had said about his drinking.

SIOBHAN TAPPED lightly on the ladies' dressing room door as she and Padraig stood outside.

"Come in, Siobhan, I'm ready," Natalie called from inside. The small room was full of steam from Natalie's shower after a vigorous training routine in the boxing ring. Dressed in a tight t-shirt and track suit bottoms, she towered over Siobhan and Padraig as she asked them to sit down on a bench next to the wall. Siobhan chatted with her for a few minutes about training and the work-outs while Padraig sat staring in awe at her body. Any lumberjack in Alaska, he knew, would envy Natalie's broad, well-defined shoulders, from which hung vein-engorged muscular arms leading down to hands as big as shovels. As she towel-dried her wet hair, Padraig's eyes rested on her wide neck which seemed to have merged into a huge muscle connecting her head to her body. Padraig knew from Siobhan that Natalie was taking hormone tablets, which would account for what looked like a five o'clock shadow on her chin. Padraig focussed on a spot on the wall opposite, trying to prevent his eyes wandering down to check developments in the area around Natalie's crotch.

"I hear you want a nixer done." Natalie sounded half-man, half-woman. An image of Arnold Schwarzenegger flooded his mind, which he pushed back with effort and timidly said, "Yes. I'd like to employ your services." He sounded official but felt stupid as he didn't know the right words to say in a situation like this.

"Who is this person you need sorted?" Natalie asked, slowing down on the word sorted.

"It's a man," Padraig stuttered. "I want revenge." He turned to look at Natalie who stared into Padraig's eyes.

"First, I would like to know if you want to give him a good-going over or just a warning," Natalie asked. "What kind of revenge do you want?"

Padraig had thought long and hard about this since seeing Natalie in action in the ring. He had anticipated this moment so much that he expected it to be full of drama, but now that it had happened it was quite an anti-climax. He felt calm and resolved about what he wanted done.

"I want a good going over, no police involved please," he said.

"I want him to have permanent physical scars, so that when he looks at them he will know who caused them. I want him to know that you're doing this on my behalf."

"I must ask," Natalie said, "for me to do such a thing, I need to know what this man did to you." Padraig hesitated to answer.

"Well, this man attacked . . ." Siobhan started to say, but Padraig interrupted her.

"Raped me." The words came out of Padraig's mouth almost in slow motion and hung in the air.

"You will show me this man so I know exactly who he is," Natalie said as if giving an order.

"I know the local pub where he drinks in Kilburn," he said. "We can go there together, the three of us, whatever night suits you." He stopped to think for a moment, then asked, "May I ask, please, how much it will cost?"

"Don't worry about money," Natalie said as she picked up her gym bag, signalling the meeting was over. They all walked to the exit. Stopping, Natalie said, "Siobhan tells me you are a hairdresser. So you do my hair and my friends' hair, those friends who come with me on the job, for as long as we say. That okay?" Padraig agreed immediately with vigorous nodding of his head.

They were standing outside the gym, ready to go in opposite directions, when Padraig asked, "What will you do to him?"

A smile crossed Natalie's face as she answered in a low voice, "I'm still running it around in my mind, but I do know that the kneecaps when dislocated never heal again properly. I also know that the skin around the male genital area is extremely sensitive to burns, and never ever heals properly, so much so that the man will never get an erection again."

Padraig watched Natalie walk away calmly and could hear her call, "Be in touch", as she crossed the road and got lost in the crowd. Linking Siobhan's arm as they made their way back to the flat, Padraig felt empowered as he thought of his list. "One down, two to go," he said to himself as he followed Siobhan through the front door of their flat.

"JUST HANDING in my letter, Mr Floyd, to go with the others," Michael said as he left the envelope on the lecturer's desk. For the previous three weeks he had handed in a letter protesting at the college's refusal to award him a diploma. As usual, Floyd ignored him, continuing to read his newspaper as he sat behind his desk.

Just as Michael reached the door he turned. "By the way, it's going to legal action from next week on, Mr Floyd. The students' union have advised their solicitors and they will be taking up my case."

Floyd put his newspaper down and glared at Michael.

"It could mean very bad publicity for the college," Michael continued, letting the words sound like the threat he intended. "And no doubt questions will be asked about how someone who won an important bursary could be failed by the college. I'm sure you will pass that information on to your colleagues."

Michael left the office, defiant but drained. He made his way to First Out, which was full of people all gathered for another gay rights rally that night. More anti-Section 28, more safe sex and condoms, more gay rights. He was tired of the constant battling and wondered if he would be so open about his homosexuality in Italy.

Later in his shift, the manager asked him to retrieve change from the office upstairs. Just as he was about to lock the office door behind him he caught sight of the telephone on the desk, an opportunity to make a free call. He automatically thought of his mother and quickly dialled the house number in Dunglass. His father answered.

"Hello, Dad. It's me, Michael. How are you, how are things going there?"

"We're fine, thank you very much." His father's stern voice transported him immediately back to Dunglass "Where are you ringing from?"

"I'm at work dad," Michael said nervously. "I'm just getting a freebie in the manager's office."

"So you are making a call on company time and money."

"Yes, Dad, that's right. I thought I'd just say hello."

"Well I don't think that's a good thing, Michael." His father's voice paused. "Your mother is not here."

"Will she be back soon?" Michael asked, trying to keep a strained conversation going.

"Don't you know she goes to her devotions in the church to-night, Michael? You haven't been gone that long." There was a silence on the phone. Michael wondered if he should mention Italy. It seemed pointless.

He thought of a way to make his father talk. "You working away, Dad, how's the army?"

"Oh, busy as usual, doing a whole refit of the camp, a new minister on board." It was the first bit of enthusiasm in his father's voice.

Michael plucked up his courage. "I'm leaving for Italy soon, Dad, heading there for a year."

"So I believe, your mother told me already." It was clear to Michael that his father was not interested in a prolonged conversation about Italy. He wanted to scream and shout at him, but knew it would be a waste of energy. Deep down, Michael knew that although his father might love him, he disliked him as the funny son who liked to draw handbags and women's shoes.

"Listen, Dad, got to go back to work." There was a lump in Michael's throat. "Look after yourself and tell Mam I send her all my love."

"Okay then," was all his father could manage to say before hanging up.

Michael wanted to cry his heart out, but was interrupted by a loud knock on the door.

"For God's sake, Michael, hurry up, it's mental down here." His colleague Trevor was at the door. " Have you got those pound coins?"

"Yeah, here they are," Michael said, handing him the bag of coins and locking the door behind him. Back downstairs at the busy bar, he struggled hard to rid his mind of the conversation with his father. He knew a drink would help. Maybe he could arrange a trip to the cellar alone, he thought, where he would attack a bottle of vodka.

"I HAVE an appointment," Padraig said in a sheepish voice to the young woman behind the reception desk.

"What's your name?" she said as she looked though a list of appointments.

He stumbled on his words as he gave his name, trying not to whisper. Although the clinic was right in the city centre near Covent Gardens, he hoped he was far enough away from Hackney not to be recognised.

"Okay, that's fine," the young woman, beaming a smile at him. "Now take a seat next door in the waiting room and Susan, one of our nurses, will be with you in a few minutes."

Her chirpiness grated slightly on Padraig's already frazzled nerves. Taking the first empty seat in the bright, airy waiting-room, he took a sly look around at the two other young men and one older woman there. Taking a glossy magazine from the glass table in the centre of the room, he flicked through it, pretending to read. His mind was racing and his stomach seemed to be jumping up to his chest bone and back down. What were the others there for, he wondered – Aids, chlamydia or syphilis? Since that horrific night three months ago his awareness of Aids and safe sex had been heightened. Trial by media had become the norm in the newspapers, where homosexuality was seen as being inextricably bound to a deadly disease. The older woman turned to speak to Padraig, but he was saved by the appearance of a plump, happy-faced nurse with the name tag Susan who called his name.

"Take a seat there, Padraig," Susan said in a soft Scottish accent as she closed her room door behind them.

"Never thought I'd be in a place like this," Padraig said nervously as he took a seat facing Susan's desk. After a few basic questions confirming date of birth, address and nationality, she quickly got to the core of the issue.

"Have you had unprotected sex with a man or a woman in the last eighteen months?"

All he could manage was a nod of his head as a cold shiver ran up his spine.

"I got the time off work and have to go back soon," Padraig babbled. "I hate blood and needles, hope it won't hurt." Susan had put down her pen, waiting patiently for Padraig to run out of breath.

"Let's pause, Padraig," she said very calmly. "This is a very stressful situation, but you did the right thing coming. You've taken the first step. I want you to know that I'm here to help you."

Padraig found her kindness overwhelming and out of nowhere he started to cry. Soft wounded tears flowed from his eyes as his chest moved in sobbing motions. Susan handed him a tissue, allowing him to continue crying his heart out. After a few minutes, he blew his nose and gathered enough courage to look Susan in the eye.

"We both know there is more to this than a sexually transmitted disease, isn't that so, Padraig?" She came from behind her desk and sat in a chair beside him. "I'm not here to judge you, but it's better to let something out."

"I've been very stupid," Padraig began, "careless, reckless, but I never expected it to happen to me." His voice was soft.

"Did something bad happen? Were you attacked?" she asked.

Padraig took a deep breath and then let out a long sigh. "Yes, raped," he said. The word still stuck in his throat and he could almost taste it on his tongue as it passed through. "Worst part was I knew him."

"It usually is the case, my dear, it usually is." Susan touched Padraig's elbow and held his arm gently. "Believe it or not, it's much better now that you have said it and its out. It's much more common among men than is widely known. You don't have to face it alone, Padraig, as there's a great counselling service here available to you."

"Maybe, let me think about it, thanks," were the only words that would come to him.

"This won't hurt, Padraig, but if you're ready I'll go ahead and take the blood samples." He nodded in agreement, feeling tired inside, yet felt as if a huge weight had been lifted off his shoulders. Susan was gentle, and after a slight pinch the dreaded procedure was all over.

"Here's my card with my direct line," Susan said. "I can organise some counselling for you to start next week, and if you want to give me a ring in a couple of days I can tell you the times. We should have your results back in a few weeks."

"It's a very big thing, HIV," Padraig said, his first time to speak the word out loud. "It seems like a death sentence, and I'm scared."

"You're not alone, Padraig. You don't need to be so scared, there's a whole support system in place and attached to the centre. Men and women all over the world have this disease and live happy lives. But let's wait for the results before we make any of those plans and deal with the issue at hand. Please come for the counselling." She looked directly into Padraig's eyes. He nodded in agreement, not really sure yet of his next step, but he knew he would consider what she had suggested.

Outside, Padraig felt a glow spread through his body as the fresh sunshine hit his face. He did not, in fact, have to return to work, as he had told Susan, but had arranged to meet the others at The Nag's Head later. With a few hours to kill, he popped into a nearby shopping mall and headed straight to the lingerie section of BHS to check out the new summer range. Smiling to himself, he realised this was the first time he had done something like this in a good many weeks.

Dear Mam, Sorry I won't make it home for Rita's wedding. I have to be in Milan in Italy next week as July is starting date. Will let you have my address as soon as I'm settled and you might consider coming over.

Michael stopped writing, knowing that never in a month of Sundays would his mother travel outside of Ireland, but he thought it would be nice to write this anyway.

I hope you and dad have a good day at the wedding. I'm sure James will be lovely in his new suit and Rita and Eugene will be very happy together. I'll send a present home when I get a few pounds together. Am very excited about year ahead of me in Italy and I know I will learn how to design shoes.

Again Michael paused, thinking of a saying he had often heard his grandmother use, "Pearls before swine". Neither his mother nor father had any understanding of Michael and his life, but she was his mother and he did love her, so he finished off the short letter by saying, *Send you all my love, Mam, take care. Michael xx.*

He sealed the envelope and placed it on top of some postcards he had written.

BLACK AND WHITE POSTCARD CAPTIONED 'SUNDAY DANCING AT THE RITZ CARLTON, LONDON'

Dear Fausto, On my way to Italy. I won this amazing competition and will be staying in Milan for one year to learn all about shoe design. I can't wait. I will make contact with your cousin when I am there. Hope life is good with you and you are still dancing with all the lovely ladies on Sundays. Much love from your Irish grandson in London. Michael x

BLACK AND WHITE POSTCARD CAPTIONED 'AUDREY HEPBURN IN BREAKFAST AT TIFFANY'S'

My Dearest Ernie, I'm heading to Milan in Italy next week Ernie. Saw Audrey in the shop and immediately thought of you. Hope you are settled in your new care home and being well looked after by the lovely nurses both male and female. Really enjoyed our time together in New York and hope to see you again sometime. Take care of yourself. Michael x.

Michael knew that he would never see Ernie again.

POSTCARD WITH A PICTURE OF A 1970 PLATFORM SHOE BESIDE A HANDBAG. '

Dear Finnuala, I am on my way to Italy to learn about shoe design. Won a big competition and am heading to Milan for twelve

159

months. Have tried to contact you a few times before, so hope this gets to you. Not sure of your address in Liverpool but heard you're doing nursing. Good luck with your new career. You'll be a great nurse. Please write back when you get this, send it to the above address and Padraig will forward it to me in Italy. Hope we can keep in touch. Love always, Michael xx.

There was a knock at the door. "Come in," Michael said and turned to see Siobhan appear like a film star in front of him. The beautiful figure that she had developed over the past few months from training at the gym was made obvious by the stylish black, figure-hugging dress she was wearing for the ceremony. "Wow," Michael beamed. "There won't be a man or woman safe there tonight." Siobhan laughed as she twirled to show off her new dress.

"I hope you're bringing that dress to the States," Michael said.

"Course I am, can't wait. It's amazing the money we raised, and now it's only a few weeks to go." Siobhan was thrilled at being given the opportunity to accompany the team, due to someone else having to drop out.

"You deserve it, Siobhan. You've really worked hard in every way."

"Just like you, Michael. You deserve tonight." Siobhan turned to leave the flat. "Come on, Michael, we'll be late."

When they got to the college, the hall was already buzzing with students and their friends and families all gathered for the graduation ceremony. The dignitaries had already taken up position on the stage and included Sir Greville Wilson, the Lord Mayor of London sitting in the middle together with Melvin Ross and Trudy Bowers, who presented a fashion show on the BBC. Newspaper photographers were positioned at one side of the stage, and rumour had it that seated to the left were scouts from the major fashion houses on the lookout for new talent.

Sitting beside Padraig to his left and Pearl and Siobhan to his right, Michael felt in the grip of emotion. Memories of changing into his dole clothes, dashing to college on his bike and the long exhausting nights working in First Out flooded his mind. All the hard work over the past eight or nine months had paid off. But, most of all, the battle with the college had been won; the threat of legal action had worked and, after reviewing his work, they had caved in and decided to award him his diploma. As a naive young man from small-town Ireland, he knew that the all the odds had been stacked against him in London. But he had changed since then and felt proud of what he had achieved, but dearly wished that his parents could share in his success.

Padraig gave him a dig in the ribs. His name had been called out. He sprung to life and walked up to collect his diploma.

"Well done my boy, well done," the Lord Mayor said as he shook his hand enthusiastically. "I believe you're heading to Italy, lucky you. Well done on winning the competition."

"Thank you, sir, thank you very much," Michael said, beaming. The flashing lights of the cameras lit up the faces of the college staff seated behind the dignitaries, and he caught sight of a glowering Floyd.

Padraig, Pearl and Siobhan were still on their feet cheering and clapping loudly as he floated on a high back to his seat, where he was greeted with hugs and kisses.

After the graduation ceremony was finished, they walked happily together for a few streets until they came to the restaurant in Chinatown where Pearl had booked a table. As the feast was laid out before them they chatted excitedly about their plans.

"I was thinking of looking for an empty flat in Islington," Pearl said, looking at Padraig and Siobhan. "Would you fancy moving in with me?"

"Well, with Michael going . . ." Padraig began

161

"And with me going to America, not sure if I'll come back," Siobhan interrupted.

"Sounds a good idea to me, even for the short term," Padraig said.

"Me too," Siobhan said. "Again, short-term basis, Pearl."

"That's settled then." Pearl said, delighted.

"What about Tom and Karen, won't they miss you?" Michael asked, helping himself to another serving of chow mein from one of the dishes in the centre of the table.

"Oh, didn't I tell you? Tom and Karen are going back to Dublin," Pearl said. "Yeah, apparently their friend Jack had this terrible accident and they are all going back to live there."

"What type of accident?" Siobhan asked without making eye contact with anyone except Pearl.

"Seemingly he was mugged," Pearl said. "He'd just got paid and was making his way home from the pub when he was set upon by three or four people in one of the pedestrian under-passes on Kilburn High Street. It's near where he lives." Pearl paused as she chewed her food, the others all eyes on her as they waited to hear the rest of the story. "It was a bad beating, his kneecaps were crushed and he may have to use a stick for the rest of his life. Karen and Tom are bringing him back home to his mother's house in Dublin, and they have decided that they might as well stay there. The strange thing is, no money was taken, his wages were still in his pocket when the ambulance came."

Michael noticed a strange look pass between Padraig and Siobhan as Pearl was finishing her story. He had his own suspicions about what had happened. Whatever the real truth was, he felt at least that justice had been done for Padraig.

"Lets order ice-cream," Michael said, calling the waiter, "and more wine." It was a night for conversation about happier things.

"TEA OR coffee, Padraig?" Michael asked as they found a quiet corner in the busy café right in the centre of King's Cross train station.

"Coffee, please, strong and black, just as I like my men." Padraig surprised Michael with a smile.

"Guess you're getting back to normal," Michael said as he headed to the counter.

It was six in the morning and the station was already buzzing with commuters as the peak rush hour approached. Padraig had insisted on accompanying Michael to the station, where he would take the shuttle for Heathrow and his flight to Italy. Two strong coffees and two croissants later they sat calmly watching the early morning comings and goings.

"It's a world away from Dunglass," Padraig said absent-mindedly. "Do you ever think of it?"

"Of course I do, but I suppose I know deep inside there's nothing there for me – just people who, although they have the same blood as me, really don't get me. But, as they say back in Dunglass, 'I'm afraid of me shite'. There are times when I seem overcome by fear and lose confidence in myself, wondering am I taking on too much." Their ability to be totally honest with each other was something they both valued greatly.

"Of course you're bound to feel like that, Michael, that's allowed," Padraig said. "But what you have to remember is that no-one else knows that." Padraig smiled. "And all you gotta do is fake it till you make it."

Michael nodded as he checked his watch – ten minutes to go and he would have to say goodbye.

"The girls will miss you, Michael," Padraig said, recalling the crying session at the flat the night before. Siobhan had cooked one of her famous big stews while Pearl had organised their small make-shift kitchen table with candles and the obligatory flagons

163

of cider. They had laughed and then cried as they talked of the past months in London together and all their escapades down the West End. Finally at two o'clock in the morning Michael had called it a night as he needed to get some sleep before getting up at five. Siobhan and Pearl, in a drunken, giggly state, wanted to accompany him to the airport this morning, but as he helped Pearl up the two flights of steps to her own flat he had talked her out of it, while Siobhan had collapsed in a heap on her own bed moments before. The drink had hit Siobhan more quickly than normal as she had been off alcohol for a few weeks in preparation for her trip to America. Michael, for a change, had taken it easy with the drink that night as he wanted a clear head for the morning but he knew he would make up for it once he hit the duty-free area at the airport.

"Guess you're going to be okay," Michael said quietly to Padraig. "You seem different the last few weeks, Padraig, as if something has lifted off your shoulders."

"You're right," Padraig admitted. "It took a long time for me to really understand what happened to me that night. I was numb, hollow inside. It was like an outer body experience, me being a drama queen and everything. Then I thought, I can either be a victim and be destroyed, and that evil dirt-bag Jack, well he'd have won then, wouldn't he?" He hesitated for a few moments, thinking deeply. "But then a plan started to form in my mind and I took back control. I made a list Michael and set about working on it."

"Sounds very James Bond to me, I'm intrigued. What's on the list?"

Padraig leaned forward and whispered, "Number one revenge, number two HIV test, and number three BBC."

"Intense or what, come on, Padraig. Spit it out, please."

"Revenge, I'm afraid that's something I have sorted, as I think you've already guessed. Maybe it's wrong, but it felt right to me, and I am happy that Jack is scarred for life, just like I am deep inside."

"Go on, number two?" Michael asked quickly, not wishing to know any more about what happened to Jack.

"The second is the HIV test which I got done. I'm waiting for the results."

Michael was taken aback by this but not completely surprised. "I think you're very brave, but you did the right thing on that one and I want you to let me know as soon as you know the results."

"Of course I will," Padraig said.

"The BBC, are we talking the dirty 'B' word again?" Michael asked, remembering their conversation about what Padraig had found in his clients' handbags at the shop.

Padraig buttoned up his coat, getting ready to go. "You have a very bad opinion of me Michael!" A smile appeared on his face. "Blackmail is such a dirty word, I rather like 'gentle persuasion' or let's say 'opening the right door'. It's a nicer way of saying it."

"I think a job at the BBC would suit you perfectly," Michael said with a laugh as they both rose to leave the café. When they got to the top of the platform Michael knew the time had come to say goodbye.

"Well this is it," Michael said.

"It's fly or fall, Michael," Padraig said as he flung his arms around his friend. They held each other for a long moment before breaking away. Padraig had tears streaming down his cheeks. "It must be the counselling, they tell me to let it out, not to hold it in," he said.

"Well, they know what they're talking about. Look, Padraig, got to go. As soon as I have a place you'll be over, and keep the faith," were Michael's parting words. He headed down the long platform, lugging his large suitcase and clutching the folder containing all his sketches, feeling like the homeless men living outside the train station with their whole lives in their bags. Before boarding the train, he turned and gave one last lingering wave to Padraig who was still standing, gazing at him from the platform gate.

Once he was seated, Michael blew his nose and wiped away his own tears and then allowed his eyes to close as the train pulled out of the station. The sadness he felt was now being steadily replaced by a knot of fear tightening in the pit of his stomach. He was taking another leap into the unknown, and although he was afraid he sensed that something greater than himself was driving him forward.

IRELAND 2012

MICHAEL AWOKE from a fretful sleep at seven in the morning when the waiter arrived as requested to lay out breakfast on the terrace of his hotel suite. He had battled all night long against a racing mind, dozing off for just brief periods when he was visited by strange, disturbing dreams. He sat at the table on the terrace and looked out over the park that adjoined the hotel and then to the Dublin skyline, above which clouds were gathering to escort in another dull Irish summer day. He thought of how starkly it contrasted with the previous morning when he strolled from his house to his office in the brilliant Florentine sunshine. The Irish weather, he reflected, probably mirrored accurately his present frame of mind as he faced the unwelcome prospect of returning in a few hours to Dunglass, the one place he had studiously avoided for so many years. And not just that – he would also have to deal with something his wildest imagination would not have conjured up. Receiving that letter had been like suddenly falling over a cliff into an unknown world.

166

He searched for a contact on his phone, pressed the number, and within seconds could hear the American ring-tone.

"Hi, Michael," Siobhan answered. "You caught me just as I was about to get into bed."

"Hi Siobhan" Michael said softly. "How's it going?" Years of travelling the world hadn't dulled Michael's Irish accent.

"Is it Christmas already? Don't normally hear from you till then? Are you here in Santa Monica?" Siobhan's voice was full of excitement. A short pause followed as Michael gathered his thoughts.

"Wish I was in Santa Monica, Siobhan. No, I'm here in Ireland, first time back in over twenty years, heading to a funeral today in Dunglass." There, Michael had said it out loud.

"Last time I was back in Dunglass was ten years ago to bury my father," Siobhan said impulsively, then added slowly and with apprehension, "Whose funeral, Michael?"

"It's Finnuala, Siobhan. She's being buried this morning, the first of the gang to go." Michael heard himself say the words but still found it hard to take them in. After a long silence he said, "Are you still there, Siobhan?"

"Finnuala, how did she die, Michael?"

"Cancer, Siobhan." Again there was a silence as Siobhan processed what she had just heard. "Finnuala's about the same age as us, well a bit younger than me," Siobhan said.

"Sorry to be the bearer of bad news, Siobhan," Michael said. "I just needed to talk to someone who knew her, even if it was all those years ago"

"Oh, my God, Michael, I am shocked," Siobhan said.

"Did you have any contact with her after we got to London?"

"Well, I sent her a few postcards from London when we got there. I wrote telling her I was moving to America but we lost touch after that."

"Me too," Michael said. "I wrote to her a few times, didn't get a reply, so time drifted along and we sort of lost touch."

"I believe she changed her mind about the civil service and went to Liverpool to do nursing, but my cousin told me she stayed only a year, packed it in and went back to Dunglass after that." Siobhan paused. "We never really got in touch after that. If it was now it would be so different, with Facebook and all of that, but you know yourself, Michael, back then, no mobile phones, no emails, all we could do was write. Things were so different."

Michael smiled. "Yeah, or ring from the phone box on the corner, with all the change you could get in your pocket." Michael wondered again if he should tell Siobhan the full story about Finnuala, but decided against it; it would have to wait until another time. "Listen, Siobhan, I'll let you go. I suppose you need your sleep for your morning client, some yummy mummy no doubt who has the money to pay for the best personal trainer in California to kick their butt into shape."

"You're right about the morning client, Michael, but tomorrow morning it's a TV commercial. Poppy and I are launching a new health supplement line from the gym."

"Look, Siobhan, I've got to go. The driver will be here shortly. Why don't you come to Florence? I'll send you the flight and hotel details, my treat. And I can explain all about Finnuala and the rest. We need to sit down, Siobhan, just the two of us."

"Sounds great, Michael. I'll talk to Poppy and give you a call back and, as the Yanks say, we can have some quality time together."

"Bring Poppy too," Michael said. "I'd love to meet her."

"I'm sure she'd love to come. Imagine, Michael, this beautiful intelligent sexy woman, actually loves me. I'm still pinching myself. Here I can be who and what I am. Guess all the therapy over the years worked." There was a pause on the line. "Look, seriously, Michael, take care today. I'm sure it will be hard going back there, but be strong, and I'll be thinking of you." They said their goodbyes and the call ended.

Michael's thoughts lingered for a while on Siobhan – big burly Siobhan with a heart of gold who could frighten anybody with just a look all those years ago. Her courage and talent had truly emerged in California. Now married to another woman and getting richer by the year a personal trainer to the rich and famous, she was living proof that anything was possible.

A chill ran down Michael's spine as he thought of the day ahead. He walked back into the suite to get dressed and ready for the funeral. He knew that a drink would help, at least temporarily, but thought of what his AA sponsor often said to him, "Always think of what's on the other side of the glass." After sitting for a minute or so on his bed reflecting, he felt safe.

MICHAEL HEARD the crowd recite in unison the prayers of the Mass as he entered the small church in Dunglass, which was packed with standing room only. He eased his way through the crowd at the back and stood near the holy-water font to the right, catching sight of Finnuala's family and relations in the front seat at the top of the church. His eyes then fell on the coffin placed in front of the altar, bringing home to him with an awful force the reality that Finnuala, the only woman he had ever felt anything for, was lying dead right in front of him. He felt a lump form in his throat and his eyes fill with tears. As the priest's voice rambled on about pain in this world and happiness in the next, Michael began to play over in his mind the letter he had received from her less than twenty-four hours ago and which he had read again and again on his journey:

Dear Michael

If you are reading this, I will be dead. The big C will have finally won the battle. I have told my brother that he must post this letter to you once it is clear that the end is near.

I've followed your amazing career and many successes over the years, Michael. My scrap book is an attempt to hold onto the love and friendship we had all those years ago. I've been so proud of you and have admired and loved you from a distance. Your escape from this narrow-minded, judgemental, small town has been my only envy.

That night we shared Michael, well that quick embrace, resulted in our son, Damien. I have never regretted it. When I discovered I was pregnant I ran to England. There I pretended to do nursing for a year but in fact I had our baby, put him up for adoption and came home alone. It was the hardest thing I have ever had to do in my life and it was a very difficult time for me. As soon as he was eighteen Damien made contact and my many prayers were answered. The few years we've had together have more than made up for those apart. Yes, Michael, he's your son. Damien will be reading his own letter right now. So perhaps you could make it home to Dunglass just one more time to meet him at my funeral. I have always loved you, Michael, so I wish you happiness, but ask that you can fit Damien into your life. I pray that it will help both of you to fill in all those lost years.

Bye for now.

Finnuala x.

As the choir sang "The Lord is My Sheperd" Finnuala's father, brother and relations lifted the coffin onto their shoulders and moved slowly towards the exit. As Michael looked at their faces, his heart gave a leap when he realised that one of them could only be that of his son Damien. Sounds of crying throughout the

170

church mingled with the singing. Michael felt helpless and bowed his head as the tears cascaded down his cheeks.

He followed the crowd as they filed outside to accompany the hearse to the cemetery, just a short walk away. Familiar faces, now wrinkled with time and on older bodies, caught his eye. He had seen his mother and father at the top of the church, where Alice had her usual hawk-eye view of proceedings. His father's Alzheimer's was so far advanced at this stage that Michael didn't worry about any recognition there. Even after all these years, and despite Michael's generous monthly cheques, his mother had never acknowledged his homosexuality. Some people caught Michael's eye; he nodded in their direction but chose not to talk to anyone as he joined the procession of people walking behind the coffin on Finnuala's last journey. Standing at the back of the crowd, he heard the priest say the last few prayers and watched Damien try to console Finnuala's elderly mother.

A MEAL had been organised at the White Horse Hotel, to where most of the mourners headed after the burial. As he walked alone Michael felt sorely tempted to call his driver and head straight back to the airport but he knew there was one conversation he could not avoid before he left; leaving now, he realised, would only be an insult to Finnuala's memory.

The hotel lobby had been laid out with tea or coffee for the funeral party. As Michael stood alone sipping his coffee he became aware of a man and a woman staring at him and then exchanging glances with each other. He did not recognise them until they were right up to him.

"It's so lovely to see you Michael, after all these years," Mary Rose gushed, kissing Michael on both cheeks. "Gosh what's it been…over twenty years?" She smiled with collagen-pumped lips.

"You look great, Mary Rose, you haven't changed a bit." The lies spilled easily from Michael's lips, an art he had perfected over the years from dealing with prima donnas in the fashion industry. He looked at her face and saw that it was motionless, botoxed to within an inch of her life, but she still managed to hold that bitter look around the edge of her mouth. Her diamond-dripped hands resembled an old woman's and her thin frame had taken a battering from all the dieting she had done over the years.

"Darling Michael, how are you? Or should I be calling you Monsieur Dufay now? How is all in the fashion world?" Alan's tone was sarcastic and curt. Michael tried to hide his shocked expression as he looked at him.

The nervous breakdown Alan had faked on his return from London all those years ago had come back to haunt him, and he had now turned into an overweight, dishevelled middle-aged man with a hollow, lost look in his eyes. Michael knew from regular updates from his mother and Siobhan that since his return to Dunglass Alan had drifted from one job to another, even trying a stint at university, but had stuck at nothing. He now lived at home with his elderly mother and, at forty seven years of age, survived on social welfare payments.

"Saw you in Time magazine the other week," Alan said. "Boy, you've really made it. And I read that you are getting married soon. Imagine, a gay marriage. How times have changed."

Michael thought of Franco and wished he could be with him right now in Dunglass instead of in New York where he was attending an antiques auction. He was deeply in love with this kind, loving Italian man and had no doubts that the feeling was reciprocal. He felt insulted by the sniggering tone Alan used when talking about their forthcoming marriage.

"My husband Tom has just got another promotion, now he's a superintendent Michael," Mary Rose piped in, her voice nervous and edgy. "He's moving up the ranks. Isn't he, Alan?"

For a moment Michael's and her eyes locked, and Mary Rose instinctively knew that he was well aware of her story. Her plan had worked in securing her Garda husband, but her ability to have children was denied not long after with the birth of a stillborn son and a subsequent hysterectomy. She had Tom's salary and credit card, but not his love,while he continued to find solace in a whisky bottle. Michael glanced around the lobby and wondered how he could escape. In his trips to rehab and years of therapy, along with his experience of dealing with models, he could spot a fellow-junkie with just one look at their eyes. He knew from that glazed look that Mary Rose had taken some kind of drug, probably diazepam or something similar.

"How's Rita," Alan sniped in, bringing Michael back to the reality of Dunglass. "I didn't see her at the funeral with your mother and father, suppose she must be at home busy with family stuff." Alan tried to show concern on his face, but Michael knew immediately what he was inferring. Rita's husband Eugene had a serious gambling problem, and Michael had bailed her out many times. This, together with four difficult children, ensured the gossips in Dunglass like Alan had plenty of fodder.

"Listen, guys, I've a plane to catch" Michael said as he shook their hands and started to move away. He had caught sight of Damien walking through the lobby.

"We must keep in touch," Alan said. "What's your personal email? I've tried so many times but can never get them through to you in Italy." He was talking to Michael's back as he moved off. "Stuck-up bastard," Alan whispered.

Michael headed to the toilets. He needed to splash some water on his face before he could speak to Damien. "Christ, I could do with a stiff drink," he could hear himself say in a whisper.

ALAN TURNED towards the function room and Mary Rose followed. "I'm exhausted," he said. "Don't usually get out of bed before lunch time. It's like the middle of the night for me. Hope there's at least a free bar, its thirsty work all this wailing and crying."

"Is it too early to take another tablet, Alan?" Mary Rose asked as she followed him like a child into the function room where a few hundred people were seated. Alan glared at Mary Rose

"I only got them from my doctor yesterday for you, they're a new type, extra strength but he is getting suspicious. I can't keep getting them for you." He was thrilled with the little bit of power he had over her. "Give it twenty minutes, and then take another one."

"Okay, I'll wait fifteen," she said in a panicky voice. As they moved forward to their table Mary Rose whispered, "Let's get this over and done with so I can get back to Dublin as soon as possible." They found their seats and Alan's face lit up when he saw the several bottles of free wine on the table. Painting a false smile on her face came easily to Mary Rose as she greeted those around her, but the shake in her hands was not so easy to disguise.

"HELLO, MICHAEL, heard you were back for the funeral," Michael heard someone say as he walked back to the lobby. He turned to see a well-dressed couple smiling at him and immediately recognised Cormac as the same young man he had last seen twenty five years ago but now filled out by middle-age spread and with a drained-looking face.

"This is Patricia, my wife of . . . how many years, dear?" Cormac turned to Patricia.

"Twenty one this year, Cormac. Delighted to meet you, Michael, I've heard a lot about you," Patricia said in a polished voice.

Her grey face and thin upper lip made Michael instantly register a dislike for her. With a sweep of his eyes he scanned their shoes and clothing together with Patricia's handbag and immediately categorised them as pillars of society. Cormac, he had heard from Siobhan, had managed to get his act together after coming home from London and qualified as a teacher.

"Indeed, a lot did happen that year," Cormac said. "That was when I got my first job as a teacher."

"And imagine now, Michael, he's principal there, who would have thought?" Patricia said.

Michael thought he could detect a note of sarcasm in her voice and felt that there was something dull and lifeless about them as a couple. An awkward silence hung between the three of them until Patricia finally spoke. "I'm popping to the ladies, Cormac. Make sure you join me in the function room in five minutes. Goodbye, Michael, nice to have met you."

Once she was gone, Michael and Cormac began to feel more relaxed with each other, their old sense of friendship rekindled.

"I heard your brother's doing well in Boston, Michael," Cormac said.

"Yeah, he always loved music, and now he's making it out there on the music scene. I spoke to him the other day, he loves it." Michael's eyes lit up when he spoke of James.

"And how's Pearl and the gang, do you ever hear from any of them?" Cormac asked.

"Pearl's still in London, busy with her two children. They're going to university now but she still manages to find the time to write her books. We keep in touch and I speak to the others regularly." He was about to say something about Padraig, but then a question popped into his mind, which he wasn't sure at first he should ask.

"Pearse . . ." he began to say.

175

"He died, Michael, five years ago", Cormac said abruptly, lowering his eyes to the ground. "I suppose the heavy drinking and the late nights finally caught up with him. He developed some type of a heart complaint and pneumonia killed him in the end."

"Pneumonia, amazing what gets you in the end," Michael said, thinking that perhaps Pearse might have died of Aids and only hoped he hadn't passed the virus on to Cormac.

Cormac nodded towards the funeral party. "I believe Finnuala went off quickly in the end," he said. "I heard she'd been fighting the cancer for the last few years but with her not living here anymore I didn't get to see her in the end. But I heard she had a peaceful death, Michael."

Michael felt grateful to his old friend for his words of comfort, which recognised the special relationship he had with Finnuala in the old days.

"Guess I'd better go, Michael, Patricia will be waiting for me." Cormac said.

"Life's been good to you," Michael said, nodding in the direction of Cormac's waiting wife.

"Yes she's a good woman," replied Cormac. "She gives me the stability and the home life I always wanted. I guess we're not all as strong as you Michael to make it out there in the big bad world"

Michael knew that this was Cormac's way of saying he had taken the easy road with regard to his own sexuality, that being married was a great cover-up and that Patricia gave him the respectability he had come to crave.

"Well, everyone chooses their own path," Michael said quietly.

Cormac turned to go but then paused to say, "I followed you in the papers, Michael, and on the news. You've done so well for yourself. The best thing that ever happened to you was to get out and stay out of Dunglass."

"For me, Cormac, there was just no coming back. I didn't

have the options you did, so when I escaped I just kept running."
Michael felt no guilt for his own success and choice of lifestyle.
"It hasn't been easy, but today I'm happy." The two men shook
hands, after which Cormac turned and walked towards the function room, while Michael decided that it was time to find Damien.

MICHAEL HOVERED at a distance, pretending to be on his
mobile phone. Out of the corner of his eye he watched Damien
stand beside his grandmother Teresa as they greeted people who
arrived at the hotel to pay their respects. In her early seventies,
Teresa looked much older and much shaken but with a brave face
for what was probably the hardest day of her life. Michael was
amazed as he watched Damien. He looked the image of Finnuala
in his facial expressions but had Michael's taller, thinner frame.
When the last of the mourners had arrived Damien turned with
his grandmother, moving towards the function room. Michael
met the moment, moved towards them and tipped Damien on
his right shoulder.

"Could I have a quiet word, please?" Michael looked directly
at Damien. "Please, it won't take long."

Damien had turned to look hard at his father. "I'll be with you
in a moment, you go on ahead, Granny," he said as he nodded
to a neighbour who took Teresa's arm and began to escort her
to the function room.

For a lingering few seconds the two men stood in the middle
of the lobby staring at each other. Michael extended his arm,
pointing to a quiet corner and said, "Can we please sit down for
one moment?" Damien followed Michael and together they sat
facing each other.

"I can't be long," Damien said. "I have to be with my grandmother, she needs me."

177

"I know, Damien, I just wanted a private word before we go our separate ways."

"You're good at separate ways aren't you?" Damien spat back at him. Michael ignored the comment, gathered himself and tried to chose the right words.

"Look, Damien, obviously by now you know I'm your father, well your biological one." Michael found himself stumbling even on these words but continued. "I only got the letter your mother wrote yesterday. I jumped on a plane immediately and I'm here now." Michael took a deep breath. "So much has happened in the last twenty five years to all of us, both of us. I had no idea that I had a son until yesterday. Things were different back then, Damien. I always loved your mother but we lost touch after I left Dunglass and she went to England."

Michael looked at Damien to see how he was doing. At least he hadn't jumped up and run away. "I did try to contact her but I suppose with busy lives the time passes, so I was shocked when I got her letter yesterday, truly shocked, Damien. I'm not trying to sound patronising, but you seem a fine young man and I'm sure you're a credit to your mother. All I can say is, I'd like to get to know you if you'll give me the time." Michael looked at Damien, still unsure how he was doing. "Your mother was a beautiful person and we both loved her, so all I really wanted to say to you was I would love if we could get to know each other, taking it very slowly."

Damien stared at this expensively dressed, kind-faced man who sat across from him. He didn't appear the ogre or horrible person that his mind had conjured up. Could this be the same person who had deserted her? Yet this man who sat here today seemed genuine and almost normal.

"I don't know," Damien answered slowly. "It's as much a shock to me as it is to you." Michael could see that his eyes were red and puffed from crying and he could read the pain in them. Michael was conscious that time was running out and that Damien needed to be with his grandmother.

"Look, here's my card," he said. "You can contact me any time day or night. It's all a lot to take in, I know, and my world may be different to yours, but I would love to get to know you, Damien. Come to Italy and spend some time with me. Bring a friend, your wife or girlfriend if you have one."

"I haven't," Damien said, pausing for a moment and then adding "We're on a break." Damien suddenly looked lost, unsure of himself, and Michael felt that the strong façade was starting to crumble.

"Please give me the time to explain to you what has happened over the last twenty five years. Let me fill you in on my life and you can fill me in on yours. I'm really interested, so let's get to know each other and take it slow." Michael was afraid he would sound like a hypocrite but couldn't help himself as he added, "You're doing an amazing job, Damien, and I know Finnuala would be very proud of you. I hope I'm saying the right thing but I'll leave it at that." Michael stood up, and for a few seconds both men looked directly into each other's eyes. Michael wanted to throw his arms around Damien and hug him, asking for forgiveness. But he knew it was not the right moment; if all went well, the opportunity for that would come another day.

"Listen, I've got to go," Damien said as he buttoned his jacket. "I have your card, leave it with me." He extended his hand to Michael and after a quick handshake walked away. Michael felt an unexpected sense of loneliness as he watched Damien go. Turning, he wiped his eyes and went through the front door to sit in the back of his waiting car. As they drove through the main street, Michael closed his eyes and said a prayer.

AS THE CAR hit the motorway for Dublin Airport Michael pressed speed dial on his phone.

"It's done," he announced.

"How did it go, are you all right Michael, does he look like you?" The questions came fast and furious from Padraig.

"He looks just like her," Michael said, "and yet I can see myself in him too. I must say he held it together really well, very composed." A lump was returning to his throat. "Finnuala would have been very proud of him, I know I was."

"You're one lucky man, Michael." Padraig's interest in Michael's life had deepened with their friendship over the years.

"You're right Padraig, I am. I was sad and I was thrilled, all mixed up in one. It was the strangest feeling I've ever felt. I only hope he makes contact"

"Sure he will, Michael, he's got a very rich daddy now and I'm sure he'll be curious to find out what you'll leave him in your will." Padraig had not lost his knack of making light of any situation. Michael admired his ability to stay positive despite having to cope with Aids for many years.

"I'd say you're right, Padraig. Are you up for a dinner tonight at the Savoy? Me, you and Bruce if he's still in London or has he left for America yet?'

"Just off the phone with him. He's arrived in Los Angeles, getting ready for the big awards, you know the usual director's thing, but I'm caught here in Kensington, God help me'

It was a running joke between the two friends, how unfortunate Padraig had been to be in a romantic partner ship with a wealthy TV and film producer called Bruce who just happened to own an expensive pad in the highly fashionable area of London.

Padraig had met Bruce nearly ten years ago when Bruce had done some contract work for the BBC where Padraig had worked for many years in the make-up department, which he now headed.

180

"I'm exhausted, but since tonight is such a special occasion, Michael, I'm on for it. I've been stuck entertaining my darling little sister for the last few days, but thank God she's gone back to Manchester."

"The Italians have a saying about visitors," Michael said.

"What's that?

"Visitors are like fish, after three days they smell."

"They got it right there" Padraig laughed. "I love her dearly but enough is enough. She's just bled her brother dry and headed back to Manchester. Suppose that's the way it should be with younger siblings."

"Listen, Padraig, I'll let you go. I'll have Stephanie arrange everything. I'll stay in my usual suite, have the table booked for eight and the driver will pick you up. She'll give you a call to confirm later."

"I wasn't feeling the best this morning, Michael. This new medication is playing havoc with my bowels." Padraig laughed. "I wouldn't want to have an accident in the fancy bathrooms of the Savoy, so I guess I'll bring an extra pair of underpants just in case I get a dose of the runs again."

"Just one more thing before I go," Michael said.

"Anything, my friend," Padraig said in his best drama queen voice.

"Just for tonight, Padraig, no dressing up. Leave the wig at home, okay? Like I've always said, you're perfect just as you are."

"Okay, boss. Guess I'll have to pick one of my Armanis and go all boring, suited and booted like everybody else."

"Okay then," Michael said getting ready to hang up.

"Listen, Michael, I'm thrilled for you. It couldn't have happened to a nicer man, you deserve it, mind how you go." With a click of a button Padraig was gone.

As they approached the airport Michael smiled to himself,

remembering how on the previous day he had felt happy that his life had settled into a gentle, predictable pattern, devoid of any more great personal challenges. But now, like an exploding grenade, Damien had entered his life. If he was anything like his mother, Michael thought, he would make contact soon. Time would tell. He was hopeful, and not for the first time he sensed that something greater than himself was at work in his life.

Pilgrim Quest

by Betty Clarke

I
T IS a regular pilgrimage to the Holy Land, with fifty people travelling by bus over nine days to visit the sacred sites from Jerusalem to Nazareth. For four of the pilgrims, however, the journey turns out to be a momentous turning point in their lives, and in ways they least expected

Father Michael, at 37, is the spiritual leader of the group. He is a man with a sharp mind and an easy smile who has set his sights on being more than a mere priest. After an encounter in Jerusalem that is both beautiful and terrifying, he learns that there is an even greater challenge he must face in life.

Ruth Reilly has recently received bad news confirming the return of the cancer that she thought had been cured through by a relic of Padre Pio. With a gruelling itinerary ahead, 57-year-old Ruth is worried that her health won't be able for it, but she has made up her mind as she believes that this trip could mean life or death to her.

Recently retired bank manger John Traynor, who at 55 is looking forward to a quiet, golf-filled retirement, is persuaded by his religion-obsessed wife to make the pilgrimage on his own as a way of thanksgiving and of doing penance. But waiting for John over the course of the pilgrimage are opportunities beyond what he has ever experienced.

Kathy Davis at 48 is a young divorced grandmother who lives

alone. Pondering on how fast the previous twenty years have flashed by, her life dominated by a series of disastrous relationships, she impulsively books the trip at the last minute after being made redundant from her job. She is hoping for some insight into her life . . .

Four people whose lives are intertwined for nine days, and each with their own questions about life. But, as they are to discover, were they really the right questions to ask in the first place?

26315633R00117

Made in the USA
Charleston, SC
02 February 2014